Sons and Fathers

November 20, 2014

For my good friend Andy.

David Gooch

Sons and Fathers

a novel

DANIEL GOODWIN

Cover design: Debbie Geltner
Cover image: Shutterstock
Book design: WildElement.ca
Author photo: Kara Goodwin

Library and Archives Canada Cataloguing in Publication

Goodwin, Daniel, 1970-, author
    Sons and fathers : a novel / Daniel Goodwin. -- First edition.

Issued in print and electronic formats.
ISBN 978-1-927535-51-6 (pbk.).--ISBN 978-1-927535-52-3 (epub).--
ISBN 978-1-927535-53-0 (mobi).--ISBN 978-1-927535-54-7 (pdf)

    I. Title.

PS8613.O6485S66 2014   C813'.6   C2014-902607-2
                                            C2014-902608-0

Printed and bound in Canada by Marquis Book Printing Inc.

The publisher gratefully acknowledges the support of the Emerging Publisher Program of the Canada Council for the Arts.

Canada Council Conseil des arts
for the Arts   du Canada

Linda Leith Publishing Inc.
P.O. Box 322, Station Victoria, Westmount QC H3Z 2V8 Canada
leith.lindaleith@gmail.com
www.lindaleith.com

Dedicated to the memory of my father

William Goodwin 1916-1999

"When a father gives to his son, both laugh;
when a son gives to his father, both cry."

– Jewish Proverb

Prologue

ELI

I know I'm supposed to grab you by the emotional lapel here in the opening sentences or paragraphs (or at least by the end of this page) and never let you go. I have to shake you so hard you'll be intrigued, or captivated, or, better yet, enthralled by the unconquerable desire to remain by my side and turn the pages until you find out how everything unfolds and what happens in the end. But I may as well let you down early: I'm going to smash that expectation right here at the beginning.

The day this story begins started off like any other. I woke up in my comfortable queen-size bed, beside my still-sleeping, slightly snoring, practically perfect wife, to the sound of the FM pop radio on my alarm clock. It was 6.15 a.m. I turned off the music before my half-awake animal brain could signal to me what song was playing. The curtains were partially open, and when I stood up on the creaky floor on still sleep-sodden legs I could see the Canal and the sun beginning to rise beyond the borders of the Glebe. The air was already muggy in the Ottawa Valley at that hour, even though we were a few days beyond summer. It was September 28, 2009. A Monday.

The campaign had three days to go, and I should have been on the road, or in the air, or eating rubber chicken in some church basement, while working with words. But I had been told in no uncertain terms to take the day off, so I had done so, extending the edict to my usual morning jog. I showered, shaved, and dressed, half-formed thoughts about work streaming through my brain as I tried to ignore them and plan the day ahead, even though I was not going to work. I was about to wake the three older children and get them ready for school before my drive to the hospital in Montreal. As I walked into the room of the eldest, my BlackBerry started vibrating. I always set the phone on vibrate, even though I was secretly envious of my friends and co-workers who fearlessly expressed their individuality with classical music, or techno dance, or Hockey Night in Canada ring tones. I spent too much of my time in meetings with people who didn't like interruptions, and I had always been guarded about advertising my taste in anything. My BlackBerry was already on my hip, where I'd been experiencing phantom vibrations for years. I recognized the number that was coming up on the display, and because of that I nearly didn't answer it. In the end I knew I had to, so I did, halfway through the last vibration, as I tiptoed downstairs to the family room, away from my sleeping family.

"Hello?"

"Hi Eli. It's Michael." Michael and I had been best friends when we were young, but we were now, at most, professional acquaintances. It has been that way ever since our last year of university, over twenty years ago. "Did I catch you at an okay time?"

"Yes. It's always an okay time." My polite fiction.

"Good. I'm working on a story for tomorrow's paper and I'm looking for a comment from your boss." A four-letter word that, for some reason, I'd never used in connection with the man I served without doubt or equivocation.

"Yes?"

"I'm looking for his reaction." He released the words slowly, and they dangled in the ether for a few seconds, so that I had to come to him.

"Yes?"

"Well, as the man who is leading us through an intense period of economic turmoil, recession, and transition, and who is empathizing and connecting with ordinary Canadians during this challenging time – as apparently no prime minister has done before – I'd like his reaction to the following statement: 'You know, Canadians just have to put up or shut up. They have it too good. Life is too easy so they have nothing to do but complain. And the ones who complain the most are those working in dead-end manufacturing jobs under an industrial relations structure that's lost its place in the new economy. They earn more than double what they should be making. It's just not sustainable.'"

I actually laughed. It's an old public speaking trick to tell a joke at the beginning of a speech, ostensibly to put your audience at ease, but actually to release the chemicals in your own brain and make yourself relax. "Michael, that's an interesting statement."

"Interesting," is one of my preferred words and one I admit I overuse, meant to denote everything and nothing. I wanted to preface the word with "very," but I still remembered a little bit of the Hemingway I read in high school. "I'm sure he'd have a great reaction. Who said it?"

"That's where it becomes surprising." Silence again.

"Yes?"

"Your boss said it, and I'm looking for a comment on his own words. I can only assume his response will be that his statement is being taken out of context, that he didn't mean what he said, that he actually meant the complete opposite of what his chosen words would appear to be communicating. But you never know."

"First of all, he never said that. I'm with him all the time. I know what he says." Despite myself I sounded defensive.

"I know you do. But you weren't with him this morning."

"No, but I know he would never say that." Exasperation was

3

edging into my voice. I was disappointed in myself for showing emotion, sounding rattled.

"Oh, Eli, but he *did*." Michael's voice had dropped to an intimate whisper. It sounded like he was right there in the room with me. "I have most of it on tape."

"What do you mean?"

"You should ask him when we get off the phone. But to make it easier for you, I just called your deputy. I was looking for a comment on the NDP's rather pointed claim this morning on CBC that the government is not doing enough to help Canadian workers during this time of economic upheaval. It was early, but I figured I'd catch him. I was right. Ryan thanked me for my call – you've trained him well, he's very polite – and told me he was in the middle of something and couldn't speak. He thanked me again for calling, asked me to call back later, and said goodbye. But he must have been in a rush to get back to his meeting because he never disconnected the call. It was on speaker. I was about to hang up, but for some reason I didn't, and seconds later I was listening to your boss tell the world how he really felt about his constituents in the unions." Pause. "I'm going to need your response by 3 p.m."

"Okay. I'll get back to you."

"Thanks."

I had to call the Prime Minister, but first I took the time to silently and elaborately and repeatedly curse myself for taking the day off, at his insistence, to visit my dying father in the final days of the campaign.

PART I

Montreal

ELI

A good part of the story I am about to tell takes place in 2009. Our newest financial bubble had burst the year before. Suburbanites in our fearless neighbour to the south walked away like zombies in the middle of the night from monster homes that were worth less than their mortgages. Good hardworking people in their fifties, who lived in bungalows thousands of miles away, realized they would have to work another ten years to make up for the hemorrhaging of their mutual funds. Bankers immaculate in jaunty pinstripes begged for bailouts and absolution. The best and the brightest chief executives had to suffer impertinent questions from elected officials about why they had flown in from faraway places on corporate jets to beg for money, and the names of companies carved into the bedrock of the American economy became dusty historical footnotes.

The men sitting on their thrones and rewriting the rules at the dark, gasping, fluttering heart of capitalism made snap decisions that wouldn't have been out of place in the Soviet Union. Our ideology was shredded like a disgraced flag. The man who bailed out the former CEO of one of the blue chip investment firms fired him on the spot because he had spent a million dollars to renovate his private bathroom. Executives fought to retain their extravagant bonuses in the wake of shareholder destruction, the average person received a daily crash course on financial instruments from the newspapers that were still publishing print editions, and we realized that smart people could and would always do stupid things. It was when we lost our heads yet again and also our memories of the recent past. We pitied ourselves for the circumstances we found

7

ourselves in and asked ourselves why we hadn't seen it all coming.

2009 was the year my father began to die, when his cells finally got tired of reproducing themselves flawlessly day after day like law-abiding citizens and decided to vandalize his body like barbarians with no respect for the orderly universe he had built within himself. And 2009 was also the year I became somewhat well known, not just for doing my job but also for another reason, which I will get to before too long. But, though this story takes place mostly in 2009, when I was forty-four years old, it really begins much, much earlier, when the world was simpler, when the music was better, and when politicians and journalists didn't have such low credibility ratings. It begins in 1983. And it begins – like so many stories with words, with a war between friends, and with a woman. But really, this story begins even before that – with a friendship.

Like many friendships, even like many marriages, this friendship was founded not on deliberate action or fate or logic, but on happenstance. My father liked to travel to Greece in the summer and was staying in 1970 in Old Hersonissos in Crete. One day, he stopped at a taverna in the main square, hoping to obtain directions to Heraklion, probably because it was the birthplace (or death place) of some famous novelist, or better yet, some famous poet.

There was a man at the taverna, pale, tall, thin, and proper, drinking a cup of coffee. This man had an open notebook in front of him on the small wobbly table and was chewing a pen. The open notebook would have impressed my father.

"Hello there," my father said. He wasn't the type who said, "Excuse me." "I am trying to get to Heraklion. Do you happen to know which way I would take and how far it is?"

And the man with the notebook, whose name was Philip Appleby, blinked and answered quickly. He wanted to be both helpful and intelligent. "It's that way," he said, pointing with his pen. "It's about twelve miles." But he couldn't just leave it at that.

Anxious to be as precise as possible, he added, with some gravity, "As the crow flies."

My father looked at the man sitting at the restaurant table, and without a smile or any other expression on his face, other than perhaps a shadow of pity in his eyes, said, "But I don't intend to fly." And that was that. Hardly the auspicious beginning of not just one life-long friendship but a second friendship that would last from childhood to university.

Fortunately for everyone, they both had time, and my father and Philip Appleby crossed paths again, and over the course of the summer they became friends. It was not only chance that they met that day; it was also chance that they lived in the same city when they were not spending their summers traveling through Greece. So it was that, at the end of the summer, they agreed to meet up again in the fall, over a glass of wine at my father's house, back home in Montreal.

That October, I met Michael Appleby. I was five, and he was just a couple of months older than me. And while our fathers talked, Michael and I played together and became friends the way children whose parents are friends do. I remember very little of that first evening, except for a moment after supper. I accidentally fell off the bicycle I had just received as a birthday present as I was showing off for my new best friend. I ended up spending the night in hospital with a concussion, and this being the start of the unenlightened seventies, my parents weren't allowed to stay with me overnight. Instead, I was awakened every hour by nurses, who were eager to ensure I hadn't slipped into a coma.

As the years passed, and as we grew from small boys to bigger boys, Michael and I became inseparable, and we no longer had to depend on our fathers inviting each other over in order for us to play together. We discovered that we lived, if not quite next door, at least in the same neighbourhood. I lived in a semi-detached house on Oxford, one of the quieter, leafier streets in NDG, and Michael lived a few blocks west and a little to the south, in a house on Westhill, just below Monkland. We played pick-up ice or street hockey, went bike riding, played Pac-Man on Michael's Atari, and played chess.

Michael wasn't a great hockey player but he was better than me. And Michael – always Michael, never Mike – was quite a chess player, far beyond me. We would spend hours playing outside on the back porch of his house or mine. He was the kind of player who genuinely studied the game, read the books, practised and memorized the openings. He also had a chess computer that for months on end would become a sort of alter ego. And he had played one or two grandmasters he had met on trips to Greece with his father. He told me of his duels with some of the best players in the world and believable tales about how he had put up a valiant effort.

It was during these marathon chess games with Michael that I became aware of the limitations of mere effort when it comes up against talent, and of how the most careful and excellent plans can turn to nothing in a moment of inattention or stupidity. It was also here, during long summer afternoons, that I became acquainted with the seductive pressures of time.

This was the slowest time in my life, although I didn't realize it then. How often does one have days to devote to chess? Since Michael was so much better a player, I would often spend more time thinking out my moves. This frustrated him. His blue eyes, pale behind the childhood glasses he would wear before he exchanged them for contact lenses in high school, would narrow, and he could hardly bear to look at me across the board. I would try to imagine the board three or four moves out, while he relied on time-tested principles and a deep knowledge of the opening game's logic and permutations. I played, but he analyzed. Compared to me, he was a human computer. Every so often, he would generously teach me some of the dark mysteries of chess, like developing my pieces toward the centre. Other times, he would regale me with stories of chess masters and their pet maxims, like, "The one who wins in chess is the one who makes the second-to-last-mistake." But he would also grow impatient with the amount of time I took to decide my moves, and one day he made a point of bringing out a chess clock. It was on that day that a slow game, a long, intense battle of wills, became something entirely different for me: a race against time. And it was perhaps fitting for me that I lost that game because I ran out of time. I refused to play again with a chess clock.

You can tell a lot about a person by how he plays chess. If he deploys his queen too much in the opening moves and leaves his other pieces undeveloped, he is usually a poor team player – a micromanager who doesn't trust others. If he resigns once he makes a fatal or near-fatal mistake, convinced he cannot win unless his opponent makes an equally catastrophic error, he is impatient, lacks nerve, and lacks self-confidence. On the other hand, if every time he makes a major mistake he insists on playing to the bitter end, hoping for his opponent to make the last mistake of the game, he is either a determined winner with an unconquerable will or else foolish. It was during a game of chess that Michael, probably when I was taking too long to move, asked me, partly out of curiosity, partly to distract me, "Do you play to win, or do you play not to lose?"

Michael was precise and logical, and he hated to lose. He was hard on himself when he made a mistake. But it was clear that he played to win. And it was at that moment that I realized I wasn't good enough to play to win – to be aggressive, to take big risks, to mobilize my pieces for stunning attacks; I had to play not to lose. Carefully, cautiously, looking for that small mistake made by my opponent, I would seize an opportunity, slowly and patiently carving out a slight advantage and inexorably widening it until victory.

11

Years later, when we put away our games and became adversaries in grown-up ways, I would often think back to those long chess games in the unforgiving Montreal summer sun.

In 1983, Michael and I started university, which brings us closer to the beginning of this story. But before we get to that, there's one important fact about our fathers that I neglected to mention, although you might have guessed it if you had been paying attention to how our fathers met. Both Michael's father and my own were writers. But different kinds of writers. I'll probably get to this later, but in case I don't, as far as my father was concerned there was a strict hierarchy of writers, sort of like the pecking order of angels in heaven or the caste system in India. On the lowest rung were the writers whose lives were entirely based on and bound by facts, like journalists, essayists, and academics. Biographers were a step above because they dealt with character and allowed their imaginations at least a little freedom to roam. Then came the novelists, who created a whole world between the covers of a miracle called a book. But at the summit, in the rarefied air of words and images, were the poets. It was the poets who worked their magic on almost pure imagination. It was the poets who sat at God's right hand and took notes.

What made things potentially more interesting was that my father was a poet and Michael's dad was an academic. He was a professor of Canadian Literature, a scholar, an award-winning writer of literary criticism. As so often happens, their career trajectories had followed inverse paths in a literary mountain-climbing version of Aesop's fable about the tortoise and the hare.

Michael's father began as a child prodigy, or at least, a university one. He had published his undergraduate thesis as a book in 1961 at the age of twenty-one with the newly opened McGill University Press, to critical acclaim and success, if critical acclaim meant a positive review in *The Fiddlehead*, and success meant sales of over five hundred copies. But he had been hailed as the next great thing by the literary academy, and his star had blazed brightly. He did an MA, and before his thesis defence was underway he'd been offered a job teaching Canadian Literature (in English) at the Université de Montréal.

My father, on the other hand, never graduated from university and never published a single line of verse until he was thirty. Although it was far from true, he sometimes joked that he didn't learn to read until he was twenty-five. While Michael's father was wowing his English Lit profs with his essays on the Canadian poets of the fifties, my father was driving a bus on the streets of Montreal. But my father had a secret life.

I remember coming home from school one day in 1972 — we all walked to school in those days without fear of kidnappers or worse — to find my parents screaming at each other. My mother's eyes were swollen, and she had obviously been crying. My father's eyes were bright, and he too was raising his voice. Both looked indignant, as though each was sure of having suffered the greater betrayal. When my father saw me, he shook his head and left the room. I went over to my mother and put my arms around her until she stopped sobbing.

I soon noticed my father was hanging around the house much more than he used to. He was there in the morning when I woke up, he was there in the afternoon when I came home from school, and he was there at night when I went to bed. It wasn't as if he gave me breakfast or milk and cookies after school or even put me to bed — all that remained the responsibility of my mother — but he was at home. Still my mother and father refused to tell me what they had been fighting about. It wasn't until a few years later that I was able to piece it together, while reading an interview with my father after he won his first Governor General's Award for Poetry. His interviews carried more weight as he began to become famous — and famous like a rock star or a politician or even a hockey player, not like a poet. What sounded like an off-the-cuff, impromptu anecdote, filled with a lot of self-deprecating laughter, became part of the accepted legend.

My father had won a scholarship to McGill in 1955, although he didn't need one. His father, my grandfather, had wanted him to study business and take over Tredman's, the family clothing business. My grandfather was a Jewish immigrant from Russia who, like so many immigrants at the time – this was in 1927 – had come here with nothing. With only desire and the will that sometimes comes from starting over with nothing on a new continent, he had, within the space of ten years, taught himself a serviceable if accented English, opened up his men's fine clothing factory on the Main, and bought himself a place in the Anglo-Saxon upper middle class, not only figuratively but also in the form of a stone mansion in Westmount, on the north side of The Boulevard overlooking Murray Hill Park and the sprawling city below. And if his dreams for his son had been followed, everything would have turned out differently. But my father rebelled early. He had always enjoyed books more than numbers, and started to write poetry in high school. In his first semester at university, he began skipping his economics classes to hang out in local coffee shops to write. Halfway through that first year, at the beginning of 1956, he decided to drop out of McGill. His father was infuriated, interpreting his decision as a deliberate affront, and clumsily and dramatically threatened to disinherit him. This made my father even more determined.

So my father, born into Westmount privilege, left university and his beautiful family home, rented a one-room apartment on the Main three blocks south of his father's factory, and took a job as a bus driver. Most of his friends were taking degrees in business and law and medicine, and continuing the quiet, subtle inheritance of wealth and social privilege. The odd one with literary aspirations was studying English literature and writing academic essays before reluctantly taking up the mantle of family expectations. In the late 1950s, as trams gave way to buses in Montreal, and as Quebec inched toward the Quiet Revolution, my father was driving a city bus so that he could save his energy for his off-hours, when he would spend any non-sleeping and eating hours reading or writing poetry. "Perfecting his craft" is how he summed it up in more than one interview. And so he spent the next sixteen years of his life driving a bus and writing. Anybody who thought he was an overnight success should have spent just one week with him to see how disciplined he was. And that was the best advice he could give young writers: "Just read and write, and eliminate any other distractions, including a career that takes up too much mental space or requires too much of a commitment." But while he was doing nothing but driving, reading, and writing, he was in fact doing a few other things like falling in love, getting married, and having children.

He met Naomi at Pam Pam on Stanley near McGill in 1960, when he was twenty-three. She was a second-year English student, five years younger and two inches taller than him, and by this time my father had been driving buses for almost five years. They watched each other for weeks across the crowded tables when the other wasn't looking, and finally my father worked up the courage to stop by her table. "I see you're reading Conrad. He's pretty good, isn't he?" My father had noticed my mother was reading *Lord Jim* that particular week, and he had arranged to be coincidentally and conspicuously carrying the same book when he first spoke to her.

Naomi, who dressed well for a student and who, if you can trust my father's somewhat exuberant poem on the topic, looked that day like a cross between the Mona Lisa and Salome, didn't want to make it too easy for my father. So she smiled up at him, and said, "Not bad. But I prefer *Nostromo* to *Lord Jim*."

The two people who would become my parents debated Conrad

and the relative merits of *Nostromo* and *Lord Jim* for two hours, and two years later they were married. I was born in 1965, and when I started grade one my mother returned to university, where she earned an MA and a PhD in English. My father continued to drive a bus. It turns out, and this was part of the self-mythologizing that my father became so good at in his middle years as his literary star burned so brightly, that the day my father dropped out of university and was disowned, he had given himself a deadline: publish a book with a real publisher (not a vanity press) by his thirty-fifth birthday – a year before the age at which Byron died – or give up the literary life. He didn't know if he would stay a bus driver for the rest of his life or go back to university if he missed his deadline. But he did know he would never write another line of poetry again.

The story behind my parents' big fight was there for me and millions of other Canadians to read one day in the pages of *The Mail and Post*. Two days before my father turned thirty-five, which would have been February 24, 1972, he received a letter from a small but prestigious-in-a-literary-sort-of-way publisher informing him that they would be "honoured" to bring out his first book of poems. My mother should have been happy, and there should have been no argument, but what started my mother crying and caused my father to walk out of the room was what my father told her after blurting out the good news. He was going to quit his job as a bus driver. This would not have been so bad on its own, but he added that he was not going to take any other job.

It was the second biggest decision of his life (after dropping out of university and out of his father's life) and he wanted Naomi's support. He was going to concentrate full-time on writing, now that he could officially call himself a poet. With his first book, he could now take his place among the elect. The interviewer asked my father what he would have done if he hadn't received the letter from the publisher before his thirty-fifth birthday. My father looked him straight in the eye and without any hesitation said, "I would have thrown away my pen."

The interviewer couldn't help falling all over himself by writing, "I think I speak for all Canadians who love literature when I say I am so happy that Adam Tredman, arguably Canada's greatest living poet, received that letter." Before the interview, my father hadn't told a soul, not even my mother, about his promise to himself. That fact was of course important to the journalist who got to report the news, which became gospel in the ever-expanding story of my father's emergence as a writer. Not just a writer but "a bona-fide genius of the craft."

After my father became a real poet in his own estimation, things changed around the house. This was real life and not part of the carefully constructed mythology that my father had taken to using in public, so our day-to-day life never made it into any of the interviews in which my father gave his interlocutor a window into the soul of the great poet. Nonetheless, the change was very real.

Up to that point, my father had been diffident about his writing: sneaking it in after my mother and I were asleep or before we were awake, never speaking about his poetry with his family or friends. While he was scratching out a few lines, any of us could call to him for help or just to play, and he would come running. But after his first book was published, his sense of his own importance changed. My father had always shared a small room in the house as a study with my mother, but the day his first book came out he took it over as an animal takes over its den. He was less shy about disappearing into his study when we were awake, and less unwilling to tell us he was in full poetic flight and couldn't take time out to throw a ball around.

And so it was that I took up poetry in my teens just as the son of the mechanic takes up repairing cars. I published the odd poem in student magazines, and every so often my father would give me a compliment. When most of my friends were driving around in their parents' cars with the windows rolled down and Led Zeppelin or Supertramp blaring on the radio, I was sitting on my back porch reading Byron aloud and memorizing poetry. I thought I was pretty cool. It was only a few years later that I realized I didn't know much about anything I was writing about – i.e., life – and, worse still, I was hopelessly unoriginal, unwittingly repeating my father's cadences and surrealistic images. So it goes when you're the son of a great man. But I am getting ahead of myself.

MICHAEL

It still doesn't make perfect sense to me, and that hurts because I'm a slave to logic, but ever since I can remember I was envious of Eli. From the very first day I met him, when we were five years old, and I pushed him off his new red bicycle. There was something about him. A sense of calmness, of ambivalence. The subdued good looks and way of talking that owed a lot to his mother, so that he seemed a second-generation version of his father's brash handsomeness. Maybe it was the sneaking suspicion I soon had that Eli was not really trying at the chessboard or in his poetry that brought out the worst in me. It was never clear to me why I would envy him anything, because I could do most things better than him: chess, pick-up street hockey, ice hockey, writing. (After all, I would be the one who would go on to write books.) But how could it be otherwise? I envied him something he had no control over: his father.

If there were blind taste tests for poetry, as there are for soft drinks, Adam Tredman would have won hands down in most Canadian cities. He was both the greatest and the most popular poet in Canada in the seventies, eighties, nineties, and the first decade of the twenty-first century. [He would win the Governor General's Award for Poetry three times, once in 1977, once in 1984, and once again in 2005. A fucking poetic trifecta. And when he wasn't winning GGs, he was appearing regularly on TV, where the cameras loved him.] Although he earned his keep through his words, an undeniable aspect of his magic was his looks. Nature had cast him against type. He didn't look like a poet. In Canada, poets are mostly invisible except when one of them is blubbering away on stage about the rarefied rewards of the poetic life while accepting a pseudo-substantial literary prize or pasting their verses up on buses courtesy of some city bureaucrat's sudden brainwave to promote literary culture. When you do observe the shadows of poets flitting across our cultural stage, they're supposed to be skinny and pale and maybe even wear glasses – easy to miss between Britney Spears's kinetic antics and astoundingly expensive movies based on comic books.

Adam Tredman looked like a wrestler. He wasn't tall, about five nine, and his chest and shoulders and curly black chest hair were always popping out of his tight white T-shirts. He combed his black hair straight back like Robert De Niro or one of those real mobsters in the thirties. And he never spoke quietly. Every word was a gunshot, every sentence a pronunciation – or, at the very least, a declaration. When he was talking about poetry, he spoke like an Old Testament prophet, full of assurance.

Unlike an Old Testament prophet, Adam Tredman swore with abandon and nonchalance. But he somehow made every "fuck" sound intellectual, which pleased my adolescent ears. I never knew "fuck" or its gerund could be applied in conversation in so many different ways. There was the throwaway exasperated "For fuck's sake, Phil," whenever he got impatient with my dad. (He was the only person who called my dad Phil. My dad was Philip to everyone else.) And there was the amplifying adverb, as in so and so is "fucking good." Adam Tredman wasn't one of those writers afraid to praise the competition. Lots of writers were "fucking good" but his favourite (in a somewhat uninspired way), was Shakespeare, as in, "That fucking Willy. He's so fucking good."

There was the two syllable "fu-uck," pronounced like a southerner drawling out his vowels and usually deployed to denote ordinary disbelief, as when he heard about the Jim Jones massacre in 1978 in which everybody sat around in the jungle and drank cyanide-laced fruit punch in a giant anti-Kumbaya. Finally, there was the soft, wispy, almost whistley "fuck," uttered barely above a whisper that signaled his complete, encompassing inability to comprehend the human species, like when he was reading a book about the concentration camp experiments the Nazis conducted on twins. Before I met Adam Tredman, I thought only sailors swore. At least that was the way it was in the books I was starting to read. His swearing made almost as big an impression on me as his poetry.

And then there was his religion, which, so far as I could tell, was an essential part of him but went mostly unobserved. He and his family were the first Jews I had ever known, and for the longest time I thought all Jews must be like Adam Tredman, speaking as if they'd all just walked out of the desert and were making up for lost time. (I remember being disappointed when I met a few more Jews at McGill and realized this was not the case.) When our families got together for dinner, I would try to sit close to Adam Tredman and my dad for as long as I could, so I could listen to their conversation. This used to frustrate Eli, and eventually he'd drag me away, usually to a game of chess where I would usually beat him. As far as I knew, my fascination with Eli's father was not reciprocated. Eli treated my dad like anyone else's.

My dad was the opposite of Adam Tredman. He was a tall, skinny, pale, and well-spoken Anglo-Saxon. He was a handsome example of his type, but as I got older and started to pay more attention to people's appearance, I couldn't help thinking that, next to Adam Tredman, my dad looked like a girl. He usually spoke in complete paragraphs, and I never heard him end a sentence with a preposition, but my dad wasn't a poet or even a novelist. Although Eli's father never seemed to hold it against him, my dad was planted firmly on the lowest rung in Tredman's hierarchy of writers: he was an academic. And for the longest time, he was writing a biography of Adam Tredman.

When we were visiting the Tredmans, I couldn't bear to be out of earshot of the biographer and his subject. I would sometimes

21

pretend I'd forgotten a book on the coffee table and then hover, hoping they wouldn't notice me eavesdropping. I'd try to disappear into the wallpaper that none of us had in our compact NDG homes while making mental notes. I did this because I was fascinated by Eli's father and because I wanted to learn about writing. I call their interactions, often over supper, conversations, but they were Socratic dialogues at best, rambling interviews at worst. Eli's father would expound, declaim, throw out rhetorical questions, express conclusions about poetry and life and art, and my dad would listen, smile, nod, and interject at the appropriate moments. Sometimes he would take notes for the biography. For those of you who prefer watching Hockey Night in Canada to listening to poets and academics trade witticisms, it was a bit like watching Don Cherry and Ron Maclean "interact" on Coach's Corner. One guy was loud and confident and full of colour and opinions, looking directly at the camera and talking to the world; the other was quietly listening, mostly in profile, offering the occasional polite challenge, the lifted eyebrow, the eventual nodding agreement.

They belonged to a book club that met once a month, but because it was held at the Monkland Tavern, which was then a bar and not a restaurant, there was no way I could attend. At the time I thought nothing of it, but nobody seemed to be part of a book club before Oprah came along. As I look back on it now, though, with the exception of the tavern location, their book club seems not only unusual, but rather feminine. [The dearth of men's book clubs and the general focus of their reading doesn't appear to have changed in over thirty years. In a recent *Mail and Post* feature on men and women's reading habits, the writer cites research that women buy eighty per cent of all fiction published in the English-speaking world. Men apparently prefer non-fiction because it isn't made up and because they can learn something in return for their investment of time.]

Unlike Eli, I never had any ambition to be a poet. But I desperately wanted to be a writer. Just like Eli's dad. Except in my case, a novelist. I would carry around a small notebook everywhere with me, making observations, jotting down dialogue overheard on the bus or metro, writing character sketches – all because I had learned that is what writers did. A writer trying to start a career is just as desperate, hopeless, and full of crazy dreams as the young aspiring actor moving to LA, but without the semi-nude modeling to pay the rent, and with little hope of any money at the end.

All things being equal, I should have been as good at fiction as I was at chess. I read a lot of books, and by the time I was in my late teens, I knew as much about writing as I did about chess openings. I could write clean, believable dialogue. I knew how to build suspense one sentence at a time, skipping from scene to scene and from point of view to point of view like a born thriller writer. In just half a page I could put the reader in a place – pick a dot on a map of the world – using a cocktail of sight and sound and smell and taste. I could breathe life into any character with a few featherweight details. And through it all, word after word, I could conscientiously explore a theme.

But for all my ability in these areas, and though I'd eventually make a career of writing award-winning prose, I had an inescapable fatal flaw when it came to fiction. It would be years before I would come across the damning (and extremely prejudiced and unfair) definition of a journalist as someone with "no ideas and the ability to express them." [The full quote, "No ideas and the ability to express them – that's a journalist" is from Karl Kraus. He was the Jewish Austrian writer and ironically a journalist, known also to astute readers of Wikipedia everywhere as a "satirist, essayist, aphorist, playwright, and poet." Kraus, who lived from 1874 to 1936, was a fascinating figure who walked out on his Judaism and single-handedly published a literary newspaper for many years. He saw language as a window into the Zeitgeist and believed that the smallest of errors, say a missing comma, signified the failings of the age.]

But the simple truth of the matter was that I couldn't make anything up.

Recognizing my failing, I set out to rectify it in the only way I knew how: logically. In my desire to turn myself into a fiction writer, I decided to turn my back on the wisdom that every second-rate teacher of creative writing (although really, what other kind of writing is there?) lacking in imagination foists on his unsuspecting students: write what you know. [In the vast intellectual wasteland otherwise known as the Internet, this quote is variously attributed to Mark Twain, William Faulkner, and Ernest Hemingway. American poet Howard Nemerov (1920-91) had the best riposte to this canard: "Write what you know. That should leave you with a lot of free time." Writing what you know does, however, work well in non-fiction, which is where I would ultimately end up. And where of course I would be able indulge my weakness for parenthetical comments and asides, for leaving nothing to chance.]

If we writers just wrote what we knew, we would all be mem-oirists. In my case, I set out to write only what I didn't know at all. I started writing short stories before I could tackle a novel, so I wrote a Jack Londonesque story about a race to the North Pole resulting from a spur-of-the-moment wager in the 1920s between two British gentlemen. Both are so hell-bent on defending their upper class honour that each refuses to back down in the face of frigid Canadian weather and other assorted existential challenges. (Margaret Atwood would have been proud. It ends badly.)

I attempted historical fiction, figuring two thousand years ago was about as far as I could get from my life as a teenager living in NDG in the late 1970s. [This was years before NDG became fashionable, when it was still dull and drab and predominantly English. It was before Monkland Avenue boasted anything above a run-down tavern and a couple of restaurants, before I'd ever heard of Starbucks and Ben and Jerry's, before the street was rechristened Monkland Village at a point in our North American civilization when slick urban marketers could dub any quaint inner-city neighbourhood that was not a sub-division "a village."]

I wrote an admittedly anachronistic twenty pages about two centurions who talked like the bad guys in an Elmore Leonard novel might have if they had studied Latin. One day at the games, these two Roman soldiers come up with the idea of kidnapping a Greek philosopher with a great sense of self, and holding him for ransom. I even tried my sorry hand at genre fiction, coming up with a story about two senior citizens in a nursing home who decide to rob a bank because their lives up to that point had been too boring and predictable.

I'm sure you'll agree that here on the page each story sounds promising enough, but every foray into fiction ostensibly far from my comfort zone ended up being about a thinly disguised Adam Tredman and my dad. This was true whether they were wearing .parkas in their race to the Pole, or putting nylons over their faces and walking into their neighbourhood bank, or wearing breastplates and skirts and sneaking drugged philosophers through hidden passageways in Roman amphitheatres. Every story featured two main characters with one being dominant and the other less so. One guy – whether Brit in the blinding snow, gun-toting arthritic bandit, or scarred centurion speaking in hoodlum pig Latin – was the exuberant, confident, extrovert: the experienced master. The other was always the taller, thinner, paler, more introverted follower, the foil, the Boswell to the other's Johnson. In the Arctic story, the version of my dad was the gentleman diarist recording the journey until his hand goes numb and he loses his fingers to frostbite. In the bank caper, the two octogenarians get away with it, but the quieter, beta bandit can't help sending postcards to his daughter from the French Riviera, where they are living the high life. These postcards are in code, but he is a bad code maker, and his messages eventually alert the police to his role in the plot. In the Roman epic, my dad was disguised as the centurion who fancies himself a philosopher and tries to write his own dialogues, and, poor man of action, eventually talks (or writes) himself out of the kidnapping scheme.

In my late teens, as I was approaching university, I started sending off my work to literary journals, and I swiftly became a magnet for rejection. Some of the rejection letters read like they'd been written by keeners who'd taken courses on giving feedback and had learned to couple the bad tightly with the good. As in, "We really like your story's ending but the rest of it is rather weak." Or, "We really liked your story and it survived to a very short list, but in the end, we just couldn't fit it in."

Sometimes the editor giving his or her ink-stained thumbs down shed all inhibitions or seemed to be trying to settle a non-existent score. My most cherished example of this sub-genre, what I dubbed the "no holds barred" school of rejection, was, "Your characters are flat, your dialogue is wooden, there is no action, and the plot is not readily apparent. If it weren't for your ideas, we would never have read to the end. This is not a story but an essay." In case I wasn't getting the message, one editor made it very simple for me, mimicking the style of those concise predictions found in Chinese fortune cookies: "You have a future, and it is not in fiction." One of my favourites, from a witty sort of fellow, read, "With apologies to Goethe: when characters and plot fail, ideas come in very handy." [The actual quote by Johann Wolfgang von Goethe is "When ideas fail, words come in very handy." Impossible to argue with old Wolfgang.]

If the author behind the form letter was particularly sensitive, he or she might write, "We wish you the best in finding a home for your writing." Some of the more diplomatic rejection form letters, the ones that sounded like they were dictated by wannabe

John Grishams – *pro bono* lawyers writing fiction in their spare time – read, "After great deliberation, we regret to inform you that our editors have decided not to publish your story. Our decisions are based on our own likes and dislikes and are not necessarily a reflection of merit. We wish you all the best in placing your work elsewhere."

My closest brush with publication came when I tore open a self-addressed envelope to read the following note: "We really liked your story. If you would consider altering the ending so that the narrator actually does go through with his divorce – his reluctance to do so is just not believable in the context of his development to that point – then we would reconsider it." I was so psyched I completely misread it. I thought I was being offered publication as long as I accepted the recommended edits and included a divorce. (If only life were that simple.) I revised the story that same day and sent it off again, only to be crushed six months later when the rejection letter arrived, from a different editor: "We prefer to publish stories that have clear character development. We found your narrator's decision to divorce his unfaithful wife to not be credible within the context of his character as developed up that point in the story."

One Friday night in 1980, my family was over at Eli's house for supper. Our parents took turns inviting each other over, but it seemed like we always spent a little more time at Eli's. Our parents had already finished two bottles of wine, and we were at least an hour away from clearing the table. We didn't know we were destined for a second referendum in another fifteen years, but what we later came to call the first referendum, on Tuesday, May 20, 1980, was imminent. I had just turned fifteen and hadn't really been following the issue. It was hard for someone who hadn't yet had a girlfriend to get his teenaged head around breaking up with a person, let alone a country.

My dad wasn't a fan of separation, but part of his personality was his ability to appreciate both sides of a debate. He couldn't speak French half as well as Adam Tredman, and when he did it sounded woefully Anglo. He spoke the way one of my high school French teachers referred to as talking with a potato in your mouth. But he came from that reasonable Anglo-Saxon tradition that had peacefully let the Empire slip away, on whose soldiers' sense of fair play Gandhi's civil disobedience had worked its sophisticated charms. My dad was sympathetic to the grievances and aspirations behind the clever and lawyerly "sovereignty association" that René Lévesque was so passionately promoting in the lead-up to the vote.

But Adam Tredman was having none of it. He actually pounded the table as he spoke – something I had never seen him or anyone else do before – and leaned forward as if he were about to arm-wrestle my dad. He expressed disappointment in my dad, thought he knew better, couldn't abide ethnocentric nationalism less than forty years after the war in Europe, etc. Surprisingly, Adam Tredman didn't swear once during his tirade, as if the potential breakup of Canada was somehow even beyond the use of "fuck." He went on and on but, interested as I was in his words, I was more interested in my mom's face and body language.

My mom worked in one of those small art galleries on Sherbrooke Street just east of Guy. Sylvia was an empowering, if somewhat absent-minded, mother. She never watched over my shoulder to make sure my homework was done or asked me if I needed any help with it. She assumed I would finish it on my own. And she didn't spend a lot of time cooking nutritious meals or cleaning up after us. (It was my dad who liked to cook and who tucked us in.) But she wasn't completely uninvolved. She did teach me how to read and how to paint. And she had all the time in the world when it came to talking to me about books or art. (As I got older, I stuck with the reading but gave up on the painting.) In whatever free time she could find between a full-time job and raising a son, she

28

painted in our spare bedroom. As a boy, I always thought artists were supposed to strip away appearances to reveal the truth inside, but my mom always seemed fascinated with the surfaces of things. Houses. Clothes. Skin. Despite her departure from the norm, I loved her the way every son loves his mother.

That night at the Tredmans, she was leaning forward slightly in her seat, watching Adam Tredman debate her husband. My and Eli's parents had sat together around the supper table many times, but that night there was something different in my mom's eyes. And her mouth was slightly open. It was like she was seeing Adam Tredman for the first time or she was a casting director who had found exactly the actor she was looking for. I thought she wanted to paint him, at best; at worst I thought something else. My dad took the browbeating from his friend with his usual noblesse oblige and, as usual, noticed nothing untoward about my mother.

It was a few years later, just before I started university, that I discovered my mother was having an affair. My father was away at an academic conference at Queen's in Kingston for the weekend. (He always seemed to be very popular at conferences.) He was delivering a paper on the manifestation of the Arctic in Canadian fiction. Even at the time — I was eighteen — it seemed to me a little like shooting fish in a barrel. I was supposed to be away for the whole weekend at a provincial high school chess tournament in Quebec City that everyone expected me to win because that is what usually happened at the tournaments I played in Montreal. The tournament started on Friday and ran through Sunday.

I took the bus up with the rest of the competitors on Thursday evening. Eli had not qualified, which was no real surprise. I roomed with a student from the Gaspé. I always enjoyed chess tournaments, because I didn't have to work to make conversation: all everyone around me wanted to talk about was chess. I won my first three games easily on Friday, but on Saturday morning, sitting in the second-to-last row, third from the left, I was taught an unforgettable chess lesson by a fifteen-year-old from Trois-Rivières who never seemed to blink. He spoke better English than I did French, and he played far better chess than I ever could. In the short space of forty-two minutes and twenty-seven seconds he dismantled me. [The name of the boy who served as the francophone Wellington to my anglophone Napoleon on my linguistically-neutral chessboard Waterloo was Jacques Tremblay. The fact he would go on to attain grandmaster status before the age of twenty-one and reach the rank of twenty-seventh in the world eventually made me feel a bit better about losing so badly to him.]

No matter what plans I came up with, his were better. He seemed to anticipate my every thought and was always one move ahead of me. It doesn't sound like much, but that one move is everything. I still might have partially recovered my place in the standings, at least to a respectable extent, but when I lost my next game I knew I had no mathematical chance of a medal. I had never lost so badly before. I had never come up against so many good players.

Rather than play out the rest of the tournament with no possibility of winning – it seemed like a waste of time – I decided to catch a bus back to Montreal on Saturday night. When I got home, the windows were dark except for my parents' room. But the light had a reddish tinge, as if someone had thrown a Canadiens sweater over one of the twin lamps on their bedside tables. I unlocked the front door quietly and went down to the basement, where I had been sleeping ever since I was fourteen. I liked the quiet and the privacy.

I was tired from the bus ride and the two losses. I slept in until about 9 a.m. when I was awakened by two voices upstairs. My mom was laughing, and my dad was also laughing, except my dad's voice sounded deeper. Happier. I lay in bed for a while before climbing the carpeted stairs to the first floor. The stairs to our basement were off the kitchen, and as I reached the top of the landing I paused. The door was half open and I could see the kitchen and through another doorway a section of our adjoining dining room. It was like the view in one of those paintings of interiors as seen through multiple doorways. My mom was still laughing and drinking her coffee, and she was sitting on the lap of someone who was not my dad. He had dark hair and was unshaven and he was squeezing my mother around her waist. At first I thought he was Adam Tredman, but even though he looked a bit like him, he wasn't. I figured the man must be one of the artists who exhibited at the art gallery where my mom worked.

My mom was feeding the man a piece of something, maybe a croissant. I could smell strong expensive coffee and slightly burned croissant. I looked down at the floor and stood there without moving for several minutes. To this day I remain surprised that neither of them noticed me standing there. Realizing I didn't know what to say, let alone do, I turned around and quietly went back downstairs. I lay down on my bed and put my pillow over my face. An hour later I walked upstairs, and they were both gone.

I really needed to talk to Eli, but when I called his house nobody answered. I don't like crowds, but I took the bus and metro downtown and walked back and forth along Sainte-Catherine, losing myself in the miniature Manhattan swarms, not seeing the people or the shop windows until it was evening and I returned home. By this time my father was back from his Shackleton turn at his conference, and my mother was preparing supper. As if nothing had happened. When they asked me about the tournament, I said I had lost and they both expressed the appropriate amount of parental sympathy.

At supper I had trouble speaking. My parents assumed I was upset at having uncharacteristically lost at the chess table. I wasn't sure if I should confront my mother or tell my father. In the end

I did neither. Instead, in the days that followed I found myself reading my mother's and my dad's faces closely for signs. Signs that my mother felt guilty. Signs that my dad suspected something. But there was nothing. I watched their eyes. I listened to their words. I watched how they moved. Everything continued as before.

There was no rupture.

My parents said all the same things to each other. They still hugged when they came home from work. My mom still kissed my dad on the mouth. What she had done – what she might have still been doing – and what she said to my dad no longer fit together in my mind. My mom also treated me exactly the same as before. There was nothing different in the way she looked at me or spoke to me. But my relationship with my parents would never be the same. I felt betrayed by my mother. I felt sorry for my father. And I felt let down by myself for not saying or doing anything.

Six weeks after I came home early from that chess tournament, a strange woman showed up on our doorstep. She rang the bell too hard, and when my dad answered the door she was crying. This time my mother was out, and my dad was home. I was in my usual place, sitting on the back porch playing chess with Eli. (I never had told Eli what had happened. I had wanted to at first, but as the days passed I realized I was embarrassed. I couldn't imagine anybody doing to Adam Tredman what my mom had done to my dad. And I hadn't told my dad for the same reason.)

The back door was open, and my concentration at the chess-board was broken when I heard a woman in our kitchen crying and screaming that her husband was having an affair with my mother. I remember thinking that neither my dad nor my mom ever screamed, and nobody ever screamed in their presence. Without taking my eyes off the chessboard, I stood up to close the back door, as if the noise inside was a minor distraction, and pretended I didn't hear anything. However, Eli had heard too, and as I contemplated my move, I could tell he was no longer thinking about his next move but was looking at me to see if I wanted to talk. But I didn't. I got my head back into the game. And I beat him.

Luckily for me, I didn't witness any more unexpected breakfast scenes at home or hear any more screaming. I am sure my father knew I'd heard the woman in the kitchen, and a couple of times later that week it looked like he was about to bring it up. But I felt guilty for not having been the one to tell him. I avoided meeting his gaze when he looked for mine, and pretended not to hear what he might have started to say. After a few days he gave up trying.

Instead, my dad got thinner and paler, spent more time at his office at the university, and began to speak even more properly than before. There were no more unannounced guests, and my parents somehow stayed together. My mom never spoke to me about what had happened, and I never raised it with her. Our charming little family unit went on as if nothing had ever happened. Except of course it had, and my parents had to find a way to live with it. Knowing my dad, he probably found a way to blame himself. While he continued to write well-received articles about Canadian literature and teach his courses, he never finished his biography of Adam Tredman. And I...I finally stopped trying to make stuff up.

My dad and I never spoke about my mom's infidelity. But a little over fifteen years later, just after I had published my first book in 1998, about Quebec's second referendum, I asked my dad why he'd never finished his biography of Adam Tredman. I had always thought that half the reason was the physical resemblance between Adam Tredman and the man who cuckolded my dad. But even if that were true, I knew my dad would never admit it to himself, let alone to me. I knew his answer would be perfectly logical, as mine would have been in similar circumstances. I assumed the other half of the reason was that his heart was broken and he sort of gave up.

Some men in his situation would have left my mom, or had an affair of their own, to get even or see what it felt like. But not my dad. He had always played according to the rules. We were having supper at a Greek restaurant on Sherbrooke Street, a few blocks from where my parents still lived. It was just my dad and me. Sylvia was away for a couple of days. After I posed my question, my dad finished chewing on his mouthful of lamb brochette and put his fork down. He took a big sip from the single glass of wine that he always had with his meal. My dad was moderate in everything, even in his misery with my mom. He smiled at me.

"Your mother and I were having a bit of trouble at the time, about which I think you knew." He brought another forkful of lamb to his mouth and chewed deliberately, like he was on one of those diets where you're supposed to chew your food for thirty seconds to slow down your intake and feel full sooner.

I said nothing. I'm ashamed to admit I didn't even offer him a nod. He waited for me to say something, and when he saw I wasn't going to, he continued. "Adam Tredman is a great poet, about which I also think you know. Like you, I loved to be around him. But as I worked through the biography, I realized his poems were far more interesting to me than his life. My words about his life couldn't begin to do his poems justice." This time, my dad didn't wait for me to respond. He had another sip of wine and waited for me to change the subject.

ELI

The first thing I noticed about McGill was that the buildings were slowly falling apart behind their beautiful stone facades. Quebec was well into the university tuition freeze that would still be in place over twenty years later, and the physical plant was already in an unseemly state of disrepair in certain areas. At the McConnell Engineering Building, water dripped from the ceilings in one of its bathrooms, and the imposing old Arts Building was no better off. McGill was still a few years away from the capital campaign that would raise an astonishing billion dollars from its alumni and friends.

The second thing I noticed about McGill was its collection of old books. You had to take an elevator in the library down to special air-controlled floors, and there you could spend hours with books that had been rescued from monasteries, universities, cathedrals, and wherever else book learning was prized when most people were either struggling to stay alive or struggling to kill others. But what made the biggest impression upon me in my first semester was the presence of wealth. The students wore their privilege lightly, like their McGill red varsity jackets. They drove Maseratis, BMWs, Porsches. Their fathers were princes, some not just figuratively. There was a girl in my comparative revolution course who spoke blushingly about her father being king of a tribe in some country, and who always had a bodyguard somewhere following her around.

I sat through many classes at McGill during my undergraduate years, but almost all of them have receded in my memory. The one that stands out is the first creative writing course I took in Poetry.

We were all gathered around the old table on the second floor of the McGill Arts Building on the first day of class. Professor Mitchell asked us why we were taking the class and what we hoped to get out of it. All of us were pretentious and solemn in our answers. You would have thought we were entering the priesthood or the CIA. But the blond student in pressed khakis and button-down Ralph Lauren shirt just looked around the room at the rest of us, dead serious, his blue eyes not blinking, and said, "I took this class because I'm hoping to meet women."

Professor Mitchell said nothing, just smiled politely as if he were being kicked in the balls but was too well-mannered to say anything about it. The rest of us forgot to breathe. And the student who had just spoken smiled and said, in all wounded innocence, "What, isn't that what poets do?" I looked around the room. Most of the other male students were embarrassed. Some because they were purists, because they felt poetry was about words, not about women, and others because they were ashamed they hadn't had the metaphorical testicles to make such a bold confession. At least one of the women was smirking. And one or two were studying this blond barbarian who looked like a university quarterback, who had suddenly parachuted into their dreams of becoming the next Sylvia Plath (minus the suicide) or Gwendolyn MacEwen (minus drugs and alcohol).

For the second class, Professor Mitchell asked us each to bring in one of our own poems. One by one, as in elementary school, we went around the table and read our work. Almost every single one of our poems was bad. Not bad in an excruciating TV-parody-of-poetry sort of way, more like just embarrassingly bad in a solipsistic undergraduate way. There was the young philosophy student whose entire poem was an elaborate botanical allegory for having sex, with stamens and pistens playing starring roles and seeds bursting into life. Then there was the young pre-law student — at least that is what he said he was, every second student at McGill was in pre-law – who also competed on the university swimming team. He had written a poem with a syncopated rhythm that tried valiantly to replicate the beat of a rock band heavy on the guitar and bass. His was probably the best of the bad lot. Mine was about an old matador "to whom old men had listened / when he was young" trying to teach a young matador how to handle himself in the arena and about courage and all that sort of male adolescent mumbo jumbo, ending with the admonition to:

Grab the bull by the horns
And twist his ears
Lest your passion turn to ashes
And break about your fires
In lies and fears.

I pretended not to hear when one scruffy Arts major at the other end of the room huffed half under his breath, "We can't all be Hemingway," and I was relieved when nobody noticed that I'd ripped off part of the cadence from Yeats's "Adam's Curse" for my last stanza.

The only poem I can still recite in its entirety was the one by the interloper, the poetic party crasher, the arrogant immigrant to our nation of poetry, the man who had dared to take the poetry class not because he dreamed of becoming the next Leonard Cohen or capturing the Zeitgeist of his generation in a few sawed-off lines, but because he wanted to meet women:

When you come to greet me, shyly,
wearing nothing but your love for me
I will come to meet you halfway
like a falcon returning to your wrist.

And when you raise your arm,
trembling ever so slightly,
I will alight and let you pull
the velvet shroud over my eyes.

Like the insensitive but imaginative joker he was, he'd titled it, "When you come." And worst of all, he read it in a throwaway voice, as if he were reading aloud the telephone number for the pizza parlour he was going to call for delivery. I could have sworn his eyes unfocused while he read – he must have had it memorized – like a rock star or athlete about to enter the arena. He was as far removed as you could be from the pretentious poetry reading voice that afflicts too many professionals. By the end of the two brief stanzas, half the women in the class were swooning in their jeans.

At the end of class, when the professor's platitudes about poetry had left us all with a bitter taste in our mouths, I was startled when our surprise poet went up not to one of the women in our class, but to me. He stared directly at me and said, "Hello," which was quite shocking when most students could have medaled in avoiding each other's eyes.

I muttered "Hello" back and felt compelled to pay him a compliment: "That was a good poem."

He seemed genuinely touched, as if he valued my opinion, as if my comment were coming from the lips of a celebrated critic or award-winning poet, and not from the jealous mouth of a wannabe poet and pseudo-intellectual.

"Thank you," he said softly, his eyes full of sincerity. He was good, gifted even at that callow age, but not as good as he would become. And so he ruined his brilliant first impression with the following admission: "I'm actually not very good at writing." As any of us who works hard to hone a talent and takes himself too seriously knows, there is little more infuriating than encountering someone with more of the same talent who refuses to take himself seriously at all. And so it was, with this very inauspicious beginning, that I met my second best friend. Not my second-best friend. My second best friend.

Years later while travelling across the country, over beers late at night – one for me and several for Allan – I asked him why he had taken that Poetry class. "Was it really to meet women?"

He snorted. "Of course not." He looked at me with those sincere blue eyes that a decade in politics hadn't yet ruined. "It was to meet you." Coming from any other guy, it would have come across as gay, but not from Allan. We both laughed. I knew that he really meant to say he'd taken the course to meet *someone* like me, but the way he said it sounded better.

"Business is different," he said. "There the numbers guy is king. But in politics the most important guy is the writer. In politics so much depends on being able to articulate a vision in a ten-second sound bite or in a twenty-minute speech when you have a lot of time, and do it in a way that makes sense to millions of people. Not a lot of time to deploy Aristotle's trinity of reason, emotion, and character. One of the things my father taught me was never to be afraid of working with people who are better than you. It's the only way to succeed. If you sift through my many talents – and Lord knows there are many," – here he smiled ironically and self-deprecatingly, but you could tell he at least partly believed it – "in the end you find one: it's the ability to see talent in others, even when they themselves sometimes don't see it, and to identify their motivation and to offer them something to join the mission. Whatever that mission is. Ultimately it's the greatest talent in the world. I knew I could talk my way around anyone or anything, but I was hopeless as a writer, and I knew I needed a writer to fill in that flat side. So I figured what better place to look than among a group of wannabe Shakespeares."

He must have been a little drunk by then, his usual professional politician's filter against uttering the whole truth weakened by the alcohol running through his veins, so I cut him a little slack. But I couldn't sleep much that night, unsure if I should be feeling flattered or used. This feeling of unease lasted through most of the following day. However, by the end of that day, perpetually high as I was on the adrenalin of feeling I was living at the centre of the universe or, at the very least, embarked upon a holy crusade, I had forgotten the conversation and forgiven my friend. What I had also forgotten was that I had meant to ask him how somebody who considered himself a poor writer had managed to write that poem he read on the first day of class. But I didn't ask the question that night because I was afraid he might confess to having stolen the poem from someone else. It wasn't until much later that I learned the real story. Allan had come up with the image of the falcon and falconer on his own. And the girlfriend who had inspired it had captured it on paper for him so he wouldn't have to show up empty-handed to Poetry class.

MICHAEL

It took me a while then, because I hadn't yet become "Michael Appleby, the award-winning national journalist and author," and because I still hardly knew anything, but by the end of our first year at McGill, I knew Allan's story by heart, at least his story up to that point. And to be honest, I can't really claim the credit, because he loved to talk. And if I want to be hard on my younger self, I'd have to say I took his story at face value, without the slightest protective Harry Potter-like cloak of cynicism. I didn't double-check sources or hit him with any hardball questions. (I am not even sure I asked him any questions.) I just quietly sat there, wide-eyed, my mental tape recorder whirring away in the background, as Allan practised his manufactured myth on the cub reporter. [To be fair, I was not yet a reporter when I first started listening to Allan's story. I would not write my first piece of journalism until my second year at McGill.]

It was a myth, but it wasn't a novel or epic in any way, at least not yet. And it wasn't a short story that could be told or read in one sitting – spooky old Poe's literary ideal – although I've summarized it here. It was almost a film treatment, more action than reflection, but strung out over weeks in the way nineteenth-century newspapers rationed out portions of Dickens. Allan told it to me in many iterations over too many cups of coffee in the cafés that grew like mushrooms around the gray and green McGill campus. It changed slightly with every retelling, like any good story, but I've edited it over and over in my mind since then, canceling out inconsistencies, ironing out contradictions, and losing a word here and there, to give it form and save you time. Through it all, Allan never lost patience. He enjoyed his own story and was very focused as he told it to me, resting his thumb on the bottom of his right cheek and rubbing the bottom of his chin with his index finger, the very image of concentration.

His father was what someone like Peter C. Newman would have called a *bona fide* member of the Canadian Anglo elite. He golfed, sailed, belonged to the Mount Stephen Club, had a country house in the Eastern Townships on Lake Memphremagog, raced cars for fun, and knew everyone worth knowing. Like his father before him, Allan's father minted his own millions as an investment banker in Montreal's storied financial district. And also like his father, Allan's father bought himself a castle in upper Westmount in his early thirties. (Unlike Eli's grandfather, Allan's father lived far above The Boulevard.)

Built in 1898, Allan's family home sprawled across a ridge near the top of the western end of Mount Royal like my boyhood idea of Macbeth's Glamis Castle. Allan believed that a man carried a lot in his genes, and while growing up he often thought that his father had bought the house because of some picture or message imprint- ed somewhere in his genetic memory: a fortress built of stone on a hill where one of his ancestors had gone to bed each night after taking off his armour and gently laying his sword on the floor be- side his oak bed.

His mother was Italian on her mother's side and *pure laine* Québécoise on her father's. [Literally translated as "pure wool," the Québécois expression *pure laine* refers to pure-blooded Quebecers who can trace their ancestry back generations to the first French settlers.]

She was the daughter of a seamstress and a union leader whose family went back to the first shipment of *les filles du roi*, the young women brought over to help populate the new world. When he was twelve, Allan's parents sent him to Brébeuf, the super-elite

French private boy's school, to be educated by Jesuits. He grew up speaking English, French, and Italian, and like many boys who learn to speak three languages, he never learned to write a single one of them properly. At least that was his story.

But high school wasn't a complete write-off. He learned how to play rugby and lacrosse with more skill than he could ever manage the written languages of Shakespeare, Molière, or Dante. He assimilated the unspoken lessons of the sports field: how to play through pain and be a team player and win and lose gracefully and all that private boys' school serious religion. It was in the classroom that he picked up philosophy and rhetoric. How to use reason and passion to sway men's minds and hearts – the Aristotelian recipe of logic, emotion, and character to inspire men with a thousand other things on their minds to an action of the speaker's choice. The funny thing was that, as awkward, as he claimed to be on the emptiness of the page, he was brilliant at the podium.

We often think that people are either good with words or they aren't and, if they are, then they must be equally good with words on the page and in speech. This fucking little fairy tale is helped along by the few writers who are good speakers and quick on their feet. In high school Allan felt like a failure every time he had to hand in an essay. It was only later that he realized how far apart speaking and writing are. Most successful writers are, in fact, barely competent when it comes to giving a speech. In high school Allan became captain of the debating team and brought home triumphal trophy after trophy to his high school's halls.

He had talent and good genes, but he also had a good coach. The best. Like Wayne Gretzky, he had his own father as his coach. Every night when his family sat down to dinner and his father was in town or home early – which, to be fair, wasn't all that often – his father would start a debate. The topics were often inspired by current events and the burning issues of the day, so Allan had to have read the newspapers – local and national – beforehand. It sounds rather civilized compared to being coached on the backyard hockey rink, but that mahogany table, which could – and often did – seat sixteen, usually left him more bruised than a rugby field. Anything was fair game: Free trade, the Quebec referendum, Governor-General's award winners, aid to Africa, the Maple Leafs and the Canadiens, McGill vs. Queen's, Medicare and private health care, the Beatles and the Rolling Stones, the relative advantages of Canadian and US football.

His father would let him speak first, and then would slowly, coolly, take his arguments apart, leaving the remains of his boyish logic on the table, dismembered neatly like the family's Thanksgiving turkey. But he learned. Before he was ten, Allan knew every logical fallacy. By the age of twelve, he was winning one out of five father-son debates. And if you think giving over family dinners to debating class was a bit rich, it wasn't any worse than Gretzky's dad. Like Walter, Allan's father was raising him to be a great one. The kind of champion he himself had just missed becoming.

[As I write this, I've just realized the full impact of these words would be lost on you because I've left out one very important detail: Allan's father was a politician. And not just any politician, but one of the finest of his generation. After having made his millions by his late thirties, Alex Keyes traded in investment banking for politics. He rose quickly through party ranks to become federal finance minister and, in the late sixties, he carefully prepared for what should have been an unbeatable run to the Party leadership and then the Prime Minister's Office. Should have been, except for the fact that along the way he ran into a five-foot-nine force of nature named Pierre Elliot Trudeau. And the rest, as the lazy saying goes, is history.]

At the beginning of our second year, Eli mentioned to me and Allan that he was writing a book review for the student newspaper. Allan nodded supportively and almost a little proudly. Intrigued and hopelessly jealous, I asked Eli if he'd been recruited by the editor. Graduate student and *McGill Daily* Literary Editor Sam Shimon sported – and I don't use that verb loosely – a goatee and a pipe, and in his photocopied author bios defined himself as a poet, essayist, and critic, all at the impressive age of twenty-four.

Shimon was famous in certain narrow student literary circles for his poetry's spare and formal beauty and the plain viciousness of his poetry reviews. It was almost a masochistic badge of honour among young Montreal poets to have caught his attention, like being struck by a lightning bolt from Zeus. He defined his own Olympian standard and held everyone to it. The flip side was that on average one in ten of his reviews was positive, and when he approved, his enthusiasm and hyperbole elbowed out his poetics. There wasn't a simile he wasn't above using in his purple prose: "Danforth's pen dangles above the island of Montreal like a cross between the Sword of Damocles and the giant crucifix standing guard." Or, "Reading Denise Lamont-Johnson is like reading the bedtime story that Margaret Atwood and Michael Ondaatje would tell each other if they shared a bed." Or, "When I read Paul Salas it's as if all the dead poets are sitting up in their crypts, listening intently to the poetic conversation."

Shimon was the Mike Tyson of the Montreal literary universe, having famously given an interview to *The Gazette* when the real world media outside the ivory tower began to take notice of him. Asked why he wrote such stupendously negative reviews, he once said, "I am a proud Canadian and I like to cross-check other writers into the boards. God gave me a strong pen and I like to use it. It makes me feel alive. Anybody who says they're attracted to reviewing for any other reason is just not being upfront with themselves." [This brutal, almost Don Cherryesque quote appeared in *The Gazette* on April 2, 1983 under the somewhat choppy headline: "McGill's Young Literary Turks."]

Eli shrugged in response to my question, and said no, he'd approached Shimon himself with the idea of reviewing the latest book by a recent McGill grad. A week later, when I worked up the nerve to approach Shimon about writing a story for his section, he examined me over the top of his fashionable black plastic-rimmed glasses as if I had just questioned his manhood or challenged him to a duel at dawn. "So you want to write for me?" He stroked the beard that gave him an uncanny resemblance to Che Guevera, and appeared to cogitate – that being the only word that will serve. Finally, as if he were doing me a big favour, he said, "Okay. Here's the story. Jeffrey Saddelbom. Ever heard of him?"

"Didn't he just publish a novel?" I tried to keep my voice steady. I was so nervous at the thought of interviewing the latest literary star to blaze forth from McGill that my knees were knocking together inside my Jordache jeans.

"Indeed. He's a graduate. Whenever I can, I like to help a graduate. He's in town promoting his book. Why don't you go interview him today."

"Okay. Is there anything in particular I should do or watch out for? Any tips?"

"Yeah, in the end there's only one rule of writing. Make it interesting." And with that, the audience was over. Jeffrey Saddelbom didn't know it at the time, but he was destined to be a one-hit wonder, albeit a mega one. He had somehow scraped together enough middle-class experience and skimmed enough of the right books to write a coming-of-age novel about, go figure, a McGill graduate who jets off to Africa to do volunteer work, falls in love, moves to the UK, hooks up with a motley group of expatriates, and struggles, with some success, to find the meaning of life. [His more than semi-autobiographical novel, *Tea Time*, would briskly sell 45,000 copies and be shortlisted for the Governor General's Award. But, mercifully, it would not win.] It was literally all over the map. But it was also all very po-mo, self-referential, meta-textual, death-to-the-author-ish, written in the voice of a subtly unreliable narrator who existed both inside and outside the book. In 204 wild and spare pages, Saddelbom had tapped into the literary Zeitgeist like a heroin addict into a healthy vein. So he had a hit novel on his pale hands five years out of McGill, and I was about to launch my journalistic career interviewing him. As I was walking out the door with my first assignment, Shimon called to me – I want to say "barked" because that's what it was, except I can't because you weren't there and you would think that was lazy writing – and told me my deadline was the following morning at nine. I looked at my watch. It was two in the afternoon. I had nineteen hours. And with that, I fell straight through the looking glass, and I've been happily falling ever since.

I'd never pulled an all-nighter before. I was one of those oddball students who actually started their papers weeks before they were due and read all their books cover to cover – and not just the chapter headings, introduction, and index notes. I wrote and rewrote until I was satisfied my prose was up to snuff, my argument transparently apparent. I was diligent, conscientious, hard-working. And I'd get A's. (Eli, on the other hand, seemed to float through university, reading his books as if he were reading for fun.) But I was about to be parachuted into a world where speed was king. Where time was reduced to its most basic elements. Where you only had hours instead of weeks or months to make sense of the world and put it down in words on paper.

Saddelbom had wanted to do the interview over drinks. Lacking much experience with the Montreal drinking scene, I suggested Gerts, the McGill campus pub. I arrived early and recognized my interview subject from his author publicity shot as soon as he walked in. He was wearing the same brown tweed jacket with leather patches on the elbows. Saddelbom was a riot. He was infatuated with the idea of being a writer, and he spoke how he thought a writer was supposed to sound. He spoke slowly, in complete sentences, with the faintest trace of a public school British accent, although as far as I could tell he was about as British as a beaver. He used the word "cognizant" a lot, as in "One," – he used the word "one" a lot too – "must be cognizant of the unreliability of the narrator, and indeed the author, when it comes to articulating the truth. With my book," – he liked that pretentious opening – "I attempt to explore the peripatetic nature of the author, indeed, attempt to locate the author as immigrant or displaced person, at home nowhere except in the world of art."

And so it went for two hours over watery draft beer. But I was young and beginning my career as a Journalist with a capital J, and I wanted to get off on the right foot. So I was objective to a fault, and I gave Saddelbom the benefit of the doubt. I edited out all his verbal and mental tics and pomposity so that when the piece was published, you'd have sworn Saddelbom was the next Saul Bellow. In time I'd learn that a journalist is allowed to have an opinion, that he has a right, even an obligation, to call out pomposity and seek the truth whenever he can. [In other words, to say "fuck."] But what I wrote that first time wasn't the point. It was the process. That night, as I went home and tried to read my notes – what a life-changing moment it was when five stories later Shimon suggested I buy a tape recorder – and began to write my story with less than twelve hours left to deadline, I found myself as a writer.

When I sat down to write my feature on Saddelbom, McGill boy made good in the dull lights of literary fame, I had my epiphany. I didn't have to put myself fully in his shoes, let alone invent a pair and decide what brand they were and how much they cost. There was no need to concoct a conflict through which Saddelbom would reveal his character and, even more happily, I didn't have to create other characters for him to define himself against. I was under no pressure to invent a setting for him to breathe and move around in as he went about his business. Instead, Saddelbom was a fully formed character with his own ready-made plot of returning to a real-life Canada from England to launch his book. I felt like Byron must have every time he dived into the sea to swim: in the water his lame foot no longer embarrassed him and held him back. In this new element of non-fiction, my inability to make up anything was no longer a handicap.

I could apply all my time and attention to the words, to telling the story, to making it real. I was like a concert pianist playing *The Goldberg Variations*, and I could suddenly focus on my fingers, on bonding with the piano, and on making the music sound alive, where before I'd sit at the piano and feel that I had to channel Beethoven as well as Glenn Gould. I had never felt so free. By this time, I knew I wasn't good enough to make any money playing chess. (Hardly anyone is.) It would take me a couple more years to graduate from doing interviews with writers to interviewing people with real jobs, and a few more years after that to work up the courage to write a book about real things like Canadian politics and society. But with that first gentle jump into journalism, I realized I'd found my life.

I didn't sleep at all that night, and when I dropped off my heavily liquid-papered story to Shimon the next morning in his cubbyhole of an office, I thanked him for taking a chance on me. He clapped me on the shoulder like I was a new convert to his church, took his pipe out of his mouth and began an ode to the newspaper business. "Journalists, my friend, if they're honest with you, suffer from an inferiority complex. You see, writers write for a variety of reasons. To make money. To lubricate their love lives. For fame. Even, sometimes, because they have to, because the work is their life." He took a dramatic pause here to puff his pipe. And then he pointed the stem at my chest. "But deep down, they all write to cheat death.

Every writer wants to leave his mark, a spray-painted simple 'Kilroy was here' on the brick wall, a list of kings and their conquests on the marble column. You write, my little abecedarian, not for those going so blindly and blithely about their business around you, but for the future human beings hurtling through the great black vacuum in a space capsule that will come upon your book and understand what it was like to be human in your time and place. For nothing short of immortality." He paused to puff his pipe and look serious.

"Now," he continued, "if you're a novelist or a poet, or even an unbelievably good essayist, you can keep the dream alive. But the journalist, he's a different kind of cat. Each day the journalist must bravely confront the metaphor for existence itself: the blank page. There's nothing there from the day before. Chances are, it's already been recycled. Every day the journalist must create something out of nothing, like God creating the world – only the journalist has to do it all in one day, not over the course of six." He actually jabbed me in the chest at this point with the stem of his pipe. "And then at the end of each day, the world disappears and he has to start anew. The journalist must confront this fear of death and failure every day, and must resurrect himself not once every two or five years but every twenty-four hours."

It's because of that short, crazy, arrogant, image-addled but still truthful speech (which I incidentally never forgot) that years later I still don't get worked up when I pick up a newspaper – mine or any other – and see a typo, the type of thing that brings out the smug grammar police who write their witty letters to the editor gleefully singling out the flaw, in the same way I'm never surprised when I hear that so-and-so has cancer. The human body is such a large living dictionary with so many words, that I am actually surprised each day it functions perfectly without a genetic typo. And I'm never caught flatfooted when I hear about its inevitable breakdowns.

The funny thing about Shimon was that he was a poet as well

as a journalist. He often told me that journalists and poets are first cousins. Obviously there's Ezra Pound's trash talk that poems are news that stay news, but Shimon's point was that both are like sprinters, committed to brevity: doing their best to carry their meaning the furthest in the fewest possible steps. Shimon was the kind of poet who could write about anything, and he did, from the childhood memories brought on by brushing his teeth before bed to the metaphysics of his preferred brand of condoms. He could make anything sound complex and meaningful with only his clattering consonants and multiple layers of vowels, like an ancient city that's been obsessively built and rebuilt over centuries on successive ruins.

Over the years, as I've learned more about poetry than I ever dreamed of when I was eavesdropping on Adam Tredman and my dad, I've realized there are only two types of poets camped out, with the occasional skirmish, along a literary spectrum: those who believe that if you say something the right way it doesn't matter what you say; and those who believe if you say the right thing it doesn't matter how you say it. Shimon was firmly in the first camp, and he never missed an opportunity to take out someone on the other side with a grenade disguised as a review, or a single quiet sniper shot delivered in conversation with an editor. I've no idea what people will think of him in a hundred years, but in the twenty years following the hothouse of university life, he would enjoy a big city writing career. First prize for Poetry in the CBC Literary Awards. Publication in all the right literary journals. An award-winning poetry book every three years. Through it all, he would keep himself alive and well and in the most fragrant tobacco with his literary journalism. Probably his greatest regret was that his name seemed always to be preceded by the words "Montreal poet," the fates of public taste and literary judgment pinning him forever to his narrow place of origin, despite his success.

The three of us were sitting in the McGill cafeteria one day in 1985, toward the end of our second year, eating pizza and drinking Coke between classes when Allan, à propos of nothing, told us he was going to run for Student Council president. Eli just nodded absent-mindedly as he sipped, but I was shocked: I hadn't realized Allan had it in him to do anything so disciplined. I think my face must have advertised my surprise, because Allan put down his slice of pizza and elaborated: "My platform will have three planks: keeping tuition fees low, focusing on quality teaching, and improving our student services."

It was clear that Allan had been formulating his platform since at least breakfast, but it sounded like cognitive dissonance to me. "Allan," I asked in my best humble journalistic way, "I don't know a lot about politics, but how are you going to improve teaching and student services without touching tuition?"

Allan just smiled, and said what I came to hear many times in different guises over the next twenty years. It was his typical response when he needed to buy time to think. As technology changed, that time would become even harder to find. "That's an excellent question, my dear Mike, but not, I'm extremely glad to enlighten you, one that I will have to answer. At least not on my own."

By then I was more than intrigued. I was full-out fascinated by the budding politician's arrogance and exuberance. "I don't get it," I said, and with that admission I was playing one of the crowd-pleasing stock roles in the media interviewer's repertoire: the gentle innocent. This non-threatening character must be diligently enlightened by the brilliant and cosmopolitan man of action who deeply and implicitly comprehends the ways of the world. (The other stereotypical extreme is the cynic: questioning everything and believing in nothing. While the cynic instills more fear in the interviewee, the professed innocent often scores better results as the great man lets his guard down, confident he has found someone who "gets" him.]

"It's simple, really. Great leaders don't have to provide all the answers. In fact it's better when they don't. What they have to do is inspire. They have to lay out a vision of the future, of what is possible. Once people have bought into that vision, getting there becomes the easy part. Because the leader doesn't have to do it on his or her own. And leadership in a democracy is interesting. A leader has to occupy a certain space a little ahead of those he wishes to lead, but not too far ahead. If a leader remains within the safety and comfort of the moving crowd, does only what people want, he's not a leader. But if he gets too far ahead, then he becomes a dictator, or," and to his credit Allan smiled then, "even worse, he gets voted out of office."

By now Eli had fallen out of his daydream and was listening. Encouraged that he now had our attention, Allan concluded: "What I aim to do with this election is to lay out a vision, inspire the fine students of McGill, and start a conversation about how to get to where we want to go. Eli, what about you – any questions?" Allan was giving a mini press conference now. Eli and I had front-row seats.

Eli obliged. "What are your thoughts on tuition fees? From what I've heard there aren't any plans to raise them."

Allan listened intently to the question, his forehead even furrowed a bit, and he paused slightly before answering, as if the question was extra special and deserved his full devotion and brainpower.

"Excellent question," he said. "You've obviously been thinking about the issue. There's no move to raise tuition fees, but that doesn't mean there couldn't be. Tuition is ridiculously low in Quebec." [In our last year of university, 1985-86, a year's tuition for a full undergraduate course load at McGill was still under a thousand dollars. Canadian.] "It's going to have to rise if we're going to maintain the quality of our post-secondary institutions. It's only a matter of time. Just walk through some of the buildings.

They're literally falling apart. Go into the bathroom in the Arts Building to take a piss, and you don't know what might drop down on you from the ceiling. Tuition hikes will come. Maybe not now, but at some point. It's a real concern for students. Someone needs to acknowledge that concern."

I wanted to add, "And exploit it?" but Eli was too quick. "But what about the fact that tuition may have to rise to meet your other two goals?"

"What about it?"

"Don't you think we should have a conversation about the need to raise tuition to pay for our quality professors and student services?"

"Eli, Eli, Eli." This was said with a smile and a hand on the shoulder. "You're a brilliant guy, but you have a lot to learn about politics." Eli shrugged, and Allan took a swig of Coke. "Do you want to know the best part about my running?"

It was clearly a rhetorical question. Eli and I shook our heads as we were supposed to. No, we didn't.

"I will have you two with me. Eli, I'm officially appointing you as my speechwriter. And Michael, I know I can't even think about messing with your journalistic integrity, but I'm willing to offer you an exclusive interview where I can elaborate on the challenges facing McGill students today and my proposed solutions for tomorrow."

And with that pronouncement, Allan was off to class. Existential German philosophy, if I remember correctly. The kind of thing where you debate how you know that when you leave your house in the morning and turn the corner your house doesn't disappear and then reappear at the end of the day when you come home. Allan studied everything. I didn't know another student who craved as much variety in his courses. Looking back, it made perfect sense for a politician in the making who would have to appeal to a wide range of people.

Eli and I looked at each other. He'd been "hired" as a speechwriter, to be paid off no doubt in beer and lifts home in Allan's second-hand BMW. [This was the eighties, remember, when BMWs were the height of vehicular cool in North America, at least among people who cared about these kinds of things.] I'd been offered the chance to sit down and have a one-on-one conversation with my political friend.

Eli thought that Allan's maiden speech should be delivered in the McGill cafeteria. Not exactly the House of Lords, or even Parliament, but a good setting for what we hoped would be a successful populist campaign. None of us knew anything about politics, but we were full of enthusiasm. Actually, strike that last sentence. Neither Eli nor I knew anything about politics. Allan, however, had literally grown up on the election trail, and he understood politics the way a carpenter's son knows wood. But Allan – and this was a large part of his genius as a leader – never let on that he knew worlds more than Eli and me. He actually went out of his way to let us lead in his first campaign, even when he knew better. When Eli first suggested the cafeteria venue, the skepticism in Allan's blue eyes was hard to miss. But he managed to look confident, even serene. He lifted up his hands as if to signal it was all okay, and said seriously, "If you think it makes sense, then I'm good with it." Even then, at the age of nineteen, Allan understood that the greatest loyalty is given and the greatest sacrifice is made by those who feel responsible for their own destiny.

Before I get to Allan's sophomoric Churchillian debut, I should probably address the question you must be too polite to ask: what was a journalist doing so deeply embedded in a political campaign? How was I not in a conflict of interest? It wouldn't have been the first time a journalist had camped out in the political backroom, debated strategy, helped to decide on action, and then gone out and nonchalantly written about it all using the third person. Knowing what I know now as a journalist, I would have excused myself from the kitchenette cabinet that gathered in Allan's father's Westmount mansion every day after classes to plot his ascent to the lofty pinnacle of the McGill Student Union. Yes, I was young, and Allan was persuasive, but I wasn't completely naïve or unprincipled. When Allan first raised the topic of his running and the possibility of my reporting on him, he anticipated my objection before it had even occurred to me.

He put his big hand on my shoulder, as he liked to do when he wanted to appear particularly convincing, and looked me straight in the eye. He seemed to barely blink. He appeared to me at that time inexplicably like a calculating bull. "Michael, I know you're a journalist and that you are bound by a highly sophisticated code of ethics. I don't want to ever put you in a compromising position. Ever." Dramatic pause. "But I also don't want to lose you. What I'm going to do for you is to grant you unfettered" – that's how he actually spoke sometimes, even at the age of nineteen, like he was an aristocrat in a nineteenth-century novel – "access to me during this campaign. You'll be like one of *Time* magazine's reporters travelling on the plane with Reagan when he was running against Carter. You will see me in action at all hours of the day, both in daylight and in darkness. You will see my strengths and my weaknesses. You will take your readers right to the heart of the political process and write the inside story of this campaign."

How could I refuse?

And so began my first exposure to political life and political reporting.

Less than a week later, when the three of us were walking up the stairs to the cafeteria, walking in slow motion in our minds, like the three heroes in a John Woo movie, I asked Allan if he was nervous. [This is a bit of an anachronism. I would not see my first

John Woo movie, *Face/Off*, until the year it was released, in 1997. But looking back on that day in the cafeteria, from the advantaged vantage point of the present, that is exactly how I picture us.] He looked at me, his face half surprised, half pitying, and said, "Of course. I feel like I'm about to shit my pants."

We laughed.

"By the way," he added as we entered the cafeteria, loud with students eating and talking and laughing, "I've changed our platform slightly, simplified it, made it more focused."

Eli and I looked at each other.

Allan just smiled. "Don't worry, guys. I focus-grouped our message at Peel Pub last night. Sure, everyone talks about teaching and the level of student services, but what gets most students fired up is fees."

And without warning, Allan was standing on top of a table in the McGill cafeteria and saying, "Hello everyone, hello, hello, could I have your attention for five minutes please." And maybe because he had a great voice, or because he spoke loudly, or because he was well dressed and his hair was blond, or maybe just because of who his father was, by the time he'd finished his call for silence, the McGill cafeteria was silent.

"Some of you know me, I certainly know a lot of you, and I hope to get to know more of you over the next few weeks. I just wanted to share with you today that I've decided to run for your Student Council president. There are many issues that are facing us today: overcrowded classrooms, buildings in disrepair, talk of increased tuition. All of these are worthy issues, but if we don't focus on one or two priorities we will not be successful, and that's why I've decided to focus on one: tuition and student fees.

"McGill is a great university, not just by Canadian but by world standards. We attract world-class professors and students. Our professors are outstanding in their fields, and our students go on to make important contributions in medicine, law, engineering, business, science, and the arts. We've all seen the T-shirts: we're often called the Harvard of the North. That's nice, but I say that Harvard is the McGill of the South." The cafeteria filled with applause. That comment had not been scripted. Allan was improvising, but he already knew, like Reagan, who had recently been elected to his second term, that voters want to feel good about themselves. "Thank you, but in all seriousness, McGill is a great university. However, just as importantly, it is accessible, unlike the Ivy League universities. That accessibility is something that we cannot afford to lose. That is why, if you elect me, I will focus on keeping our tuition low."

Obviously it is hard to be the one up on stage, but in some ways it's just as difficult to be the one behind the scenes watching with the audience. I imagine it's a lot like sitting through your young son's violin recital. You're anxious and hoping that he makes the right impression, doesn't miss a note, and has no reason to feel bad or unprepared or embarrassed.

About halfway through Allan's speech, I stopped listening to him and gave myself over to the experience of launching a political career. I was reminded of the role of talent in every little corner of human endeavour. We like to cheer ourselves up with Edison's self-deprecating throwaway line about genius being ninety-nine per cent perspiration and one per cent inspiration, so that most of us keep plodding along, waiting for a breakthrough. Malcolm Gladwell added to the mythology in 2008 with his book *Outliers*, where he came up with his catchy 10,000-hour rule, the point being that you need to spend 10,000 hours on something before you can be great at it. [My number one made-up stat about the power of numbers compared to that of words is that people are seventy-five per cent more likely to believe a statement if it has a number in it. It works almost every time.]

Gladwell singled out the Beatles honing their harmless harmonies in Berlin's seedy cabarets to support his case. But the reality is that while effort is often necessary, it's never enough. Some of us are born with genius, and those who are make it look easy. The whole spotlight on effort is the artistic equivalent of the capitalist Protestant myth in America, where wealth is not seen as the result of being born into privilege, or going to the right schools, or having the right parents with the right friends, or being lucky, or simply having a talent for dealing with money the way some can manage paint or clay. It's the result of just having a good attitude and working hard.

I was reminded of the power of words when they're spoken aloud to other people, and the space that's created between speaker and listener, like a magnetic field on an ordinary day or a new world on a good one. Even at the age of nineteen, in a university cafeteria, talking about the most parochial of issues, Allan had the gift. And I was reminded of the difference between writing a speech and making one.

When you write you have the luxury of time. You can write and then rewrite. Cross words out. Add other words in. Refine your thoughts. Speech is like walking a tightrope without a net. You have one chance to get it right. There's no chance for a redo, no chance to edit out a misstep, a flub, a fall. Speaking's like being a gladiator out in the arena, protected only by the armour of your words, your voice, your cadence, your character, the knowledge of your skill, the memory in your sinews of all the previous battles you've survived. We writers labour safely behind the walls of our monasteries like monks, with our dictionaries and thesauruses and other books, and the memory of our experiences, our emotions worn like a hair shirt to keep us eternally itchy and irritated enough to write. Writers have it easy.

Writing's an act of perpetual revision, an act of setting down and altering the past. It's a way of both forgetting and remembering. It's like having nine lives, or a second or third chance to relive your life. With speech you can try to backtrack, but the damage is already done. Writing and speaking require fundamentally different skills. It doesn't mean they're never combined, but there is a reason why there are very few great writers who are also great speakers, and vice versa. Of course, you have Churchill. And Martin Luther King. Kennedy. Men who actually wrote or at least partially wrote the speeches they made. And sure, you have the occasional writers who can look after themselves up on the podium, who can perform that hardest of all magic tricks: to appear as articulate in front of the microphone as they do within the shelter of the printed page. If you ask most journalists why they went into their field, if you scratch the surface long enough, you'll find they were shy in high school.

If you haven't figured it out by now, Allan was good at everything that counted in the lives of late twentieth-century males: he was good at sports, he was good with people, he was good enough at school, he was good with women. He was one of those guys at university who seemed to have a different girlfriend every week, each of whom thought he was "amazing," each of whom wanted to marry him, none of whom was "the right one." [In the two-and-a-half years or so that I hung around with him at university, I conservatively estimate that Allan dated thirty-seven women. And those were only the ones I saw him with. What a fucker.]

As far as I could tell, he was only not good at two things: chess and writing. Although the latter could have been a bit of a lie to get Eli onto his side, and the former I never really could have proved because we never played. He might have been a great chess player, and I wouldn't have been surprised if Allan could write well when he had a little help. It was part of his act – making people feel they were better than him. If life were logical, I should have felt envious of Allan too, because he was good at almost everything and had almost everything. But I didn't envy him a thing because we had almost nothing in common. We were in different worlds. I envied

Eli because we were similar in so many ways.

I started listening again when Allan was saying, "I could go on here for another half an hour, tell you about myself, expand on my platform, but I know you all have classes to go to, term papers to write, and exams to prepare for. Talking is the easiest thing for a politician to do. It's what we're known for. If I'm elected, I promise that I will be short on words and long on action. Thank you for your time today."

We'd carefully arranged for a couple of our friends to "spontaneously" begin clapping and chanting at the back of the room after Allan concluded his speech. Years later, to my still incredulous ears, I can clearly hear the cafeteria filling with the words, repeated over and over in young, loud, confident student voices: "If you want low fees, vote for Keyes!" Looking back and given what we know now and what we became capable of, it was amateurish. But we were young and we had to start somewhere.

ELI

When I started this story, I told you it began with words, a war between friends, and a woman. Let me skip to the woman, and then I will come back to the words and the war. I know it's a cliché, but it seems like every second story begins with a woman. The human story, with Eve. Our own personal stories, with our mothers. The story of our adulthood, with the woman who becomes our wife. The story of our death, with our wife or nurse at our bedside.

The first time I saw Sophie was at a party, in the middle of my second year at university, right before January classes started. I had just come in from the darkened streets of the McGill ghetto in the brightness of a Montreal winter. We were all young and literary and pretentious, certain we were going to be the next Great Canadian Writer. Everyone quoted dead poets and wore black and drank red wine. Some snorted cocaine on quiet weekends between writing term papers, convinced they were the second coming of Coleridge, and spoke in long, languorous sentences with lots of capital letters and allusions to the dour literary theorists we would soon forget ever having read.

She walked in, practically arm in arm with Michael. He looked like a cross between a Roman emperor enjoying his triumph and the Fonz trying to play it cool. Michael didn't go to a lot of parties – he preferred to stay home and read or play chess. I was wondering what had brought him out tonight, and then I noticed her. She had eyes and eyebrows that angled slightly upwards. Years later, I would tease her about looking like a Vulcan princess. And she had the most mirthful laugh I had ever heard, deep and loud and raucous, as if she were directly descended from Chaucer's Wife of Bath, amazed and delighted at having stepped off the page and into the world around her where she was inviting you to share her amusement for the rest of her life.

Later in the evening, after I'd sleepwalked and laughed and made witty remarks in conversation with every living ghost in the room, I asked Michael where he had met her. Not surprisingly for a guy who didn't go out much, Michael didn't seem to have a lot of dates. He leaned in, incredulous. "She's my neighbour. Moved in right across the hall. I met her boyfriend first." He sort of mumbled that last part, and almost swallowed the words with a gulp of wine.

"Her boyfriend?"

"Yeah, he drove down with her and helped to move her in. He invited me over for a beer. He lives in Windsor. Works in his uncle's company. I can't remember if it's software or real estate. He's a very nice guy."

I just looked at him.

Michael shrugged. "I'd ask her out myself, but her boyfriend asked me to look after her, in the big city. Keep an eye on her. That kind of thing."

Oh my God, I thought to myself. And tried not to smile.

Around 1 a.m., I was sitting beside Sophie on one of those old run-down standard-issue student couches. We were talking about poetry, and one of my favourite songs, "Novaheart" by The Spoons, was playing on the stereo when something small and hard hit the wall behind my head. I looked up as a penny bounced onto her lap. "I turned to see where the pennies were coming from, and there was Michael standing at the other end of the room with an intense look on his face. And that's when I knew that Michael, with all his intelligence and fortuitous tenant's luck, was doomed. She looked at me, somewhat embarrassed. "That's the sign it's time to go." And she went.

The next time I saw her was in Romantic Poetry 201. She sat across the seminar table from me, looking serious and amused. Years later I still can't figure out how she manages to do that but she does. It was the first day of classes in the second semester of my second year. Montreal was covered in a white prayer shawl of snow, and the old McGill Arts Building was dark and damp. The professor was one of those who professed more than he wrote or perhaps even really knew. He seemed too old and kind and reasonable to be exposing us to the word music of drug addicts, dreamers, rebels, nineteenth-century rock stars — adrenalin-addled boys who'd tossed off their mortal coil with style in their twenties and thirties, but at least he had the good grace to seem a little embarrassed about being our scout in the unknown terrain of Byron and Shelley and Coleridge and Keats.

After class, a few of us went across the street to Gerts, and over many beers we mawkishly, but at least loudly, recited the opening lines of Kubla Khan to each other:

In Xanadu did Kubla Khan
A stately pleasure-dome decree:
Where Alph, the sacred river, ran
Through caverns measureless to man
Down to a sunless sea.

We stayed late, and as we stumbled out of the bar onto steeply sloping McTavish Street, Sophie and I were singing Leonard Cohen's "Suzanne" at the top of our lungs, not yet holding hands, but making fools of ourselves and oblivious to the bitter cold and moonless darkness around us.

Our first date was a poetry reading. That's the un-cool guy I was in university. No movie. No dinner. No flowers. I didn't know the first thing about impressing anyone.

I picked Sophie up in my parents' still pristine Pontiac. It was one of those freezing Montreal nights, so dark and cold you could have been living in a fairy tale in Northern Europe. The reading was at the granddaddy of Montreal coffee houses, The Yellow Door, on Aylmer in the heart of the McGill Ghetto, and the reading room was crowded and smelled of wet wool and beer. This was in the mid-eighties, but I like to think that with their wide-eyed eagerness, the coffeehouses of Montreal foreshadowed the American Idol culture of the new millennium.

We had a drink and, around nine, the poet of the night made his way to the front of the room, doffed his fedora, and stood there for a moment staring down at his feet. He was dressed well for a poet, with a suit and a tie, but was still a bit scruffy looking, as though he was trying to channel Robert Palmer or Leonard Cohen on a student budget. He didn't smile and stared out at the audience with his head slightly bowed and his chin tucked in as if he were looking for a fight. And then he began:

America.
America, America, you make me weep,
You make me want to shred my pale passport
Into long slender strips of flesh, to flee
Into exile beyond your silicon shores
To renounce my inheritance.
A-mer-i-ca!

He shouted as he drew out the syllables like a man chanting at a political rally and scared half of us out of our worn-out shoes.

You have made me fear myself.
Made me ashamed to stand tall
In my red and white striped pajamas

65

On the shining white hill.
Whither art thou oh Whitman
In these songless days, these
Days not of smart men and lines
But of invasions and lies…

I will end my quotation there, but it went on in this vein for about twenty more minutes. When it was finished, he received a round of enthusiastic applause. I learned later he was an American student who had come to McGill to enjoy our comparatively low fees and European-like culture. Now, I am extremely embarrassed to admit this, but at the time I had not yet read Allen Ginsberg's "Howl," and I thought the cadences and howled refrain of "America" were utterly original. So I cut our Ginsberg copycat some slack.

That night Sophie and I became lovers, and so began what I now know was one of the best times of my life. The semester finished before we noticed, and we both found summer jobs teaching English as a second language. We painfully pretended in front of earnest immigrants that we knew as much about verb tenses and syntax as we did about metonymy and dramatic irony. We spent most of the rest of the time in bed. When we weren't in bed we were walking or eating together. In the morning I would bring her tea just as she woke up.

Until I met her I had never thought about life beyond twenty, but that summer I began for the first time to think about growing old, not alone, but with her. I thought about what it would be like to bring her tea in bed when we were both eighty, my hands jittery and mottled with time's tea stains. I tried to pay tribute to her in the only two ways I knew then: physically and with words. I was a very different person from my father, but at that time I shared his faith that poetry was a special language, a code, a mystical chant that opened magical doors. She had a better sense of the hierarchy of things.

I would show her my poems, my simple inexpensive offerings, not roses or rings or fancy meals, but black scratches on white paper designed to impress her, and most of the time she would smile and not say a whole lot. She might give me a small kiss, and then go back to whatever she was doing. That often involved tending the flowers growing on the balcony of her small apartment that I had moved into by the end of our third month together, or reading, or cooking when she wasn't preparing for her courses. Years later, I happened to be looking through an old book of hers and, carefully placed between two of the pages, I found a poem I had written her during that hot, humid summer in Montreal.

She had preserved the poem while I had lost and forgotten it; but in all her years with me, she steadfastly refused to worship at the altar of words, to genuflect and place words up on a pedestal, above right and wrong and emotions and the truth. Her best-loved books in later years remained cookbooks and gardening and design books, well-written books about real things that gave her unadulterated pleasure. She didn't seem to have a lot of time for poetry as we grew older together, but she always had time for me. She even once felt compelled to tell me, with a mixture of pity and affection in her voice, that I didn't need to write her poems to impress her.

And so, for the first time, I learned about love and about the limits of words. That words are not people, not stunt doubles for emotion, not suave diplomats who can smooth-talk you through a domestic missile crisis. That they are not children, despite the tempting analogies. That, most of all, they do not enclose a soul. And without trying to, or even saying anything on the subject, Sophie began the slow process of inadvertently changing my style. Eventually I would move away from the hyperbole and heightened tension of my father, away from his belief that poetry was the only thing worth doing with your time, away from the supreme confidence that poetry would conquer war and disease and famine and hypocrisy, to a more nuanced view of its capabilities and limitations.

It was as close to a perfect summer as anyone can have, and I would like to tell you that I took full advantage of my youth and of our time together. I did, to a large extent, but I also stole time from myself and Sophie to worry about what I was going to do with my life, possessing little more than two-thirds of an English degree, no practical skills to speak of, and, so far at least, almost enough written pages for a small chapbook of unpublishable poems.

ALLAN

As I write these words about that late summer day, I am silently thanking God for having had the good sense to create editors.
Whenever I step out unsteadily onto the blankness of a page, I feel
like a lacrosse player who's never played hockey venturing out onto
the ice on rusty, second-hand skates. I'm not sure if Eli, my favourite
word doctor, will be editing my words this time around, but I
am confident that whoever does it, they will be able to operate
upon my prose like a skilful plastic surgeon on a patient and make
me appear more adept and pleasing than I am. There I go again,
shamelessly mixing up my metaphors.

I don't remember whose idea it was to play tackle football that
September in the shallow water. I like to think it was mine, because
it's less complicated that way, but it might have been Michael's.
It probably doesn't matter. We'd driven up to the cottage on a Friday
afternoon at the start of our last year at McGill. My brother Stephen, who was three years younger and still at Brébeuf, was already
there, but my parents were away, and we had the run of the place.
We threw our overnight bags on the floor and went straight
down to the beach. It was a hot day and we had a few beers. But
unfortunately, none of us had drunk very much, so we can't blame
what happened on alcohol.

We started off playing two-on-two football, Eli and I playing
against Michael and Stephen. One very athletic guy on each team
with one not very athletic guy. You guess who was who. It was
only later that night, when I thought about the day and played that
most human game of backtracking through my memory to find

69

the signs that suggested what was about to happen, that I realized Michael had been a little manic on the drive up. He'd been making jokes, telling stories, giving every impression of being the extrovert that he certainly wasn't. In our gang of three, I was the extrovert, Michael was the introvert, and Eli, as with so many things, was somewhere in between. On that drive Eli, who was sitting beside me in the front seat, was very quiet, responding laconically but politely to Michael's stories, but barely saying a word of his own. I didn't notice it at the time, but not once had Michael or Eli spoken directly to the other on the drive up. They had addressed any comments that they'd made – Michael too many and Eli too few – only to me.

At first the game was innocent. We were playing in about three feet of water and were taking turns tackling each other. But after about half an hour, things changed. I'd completed a pass to Eli, who miraculously caught it and began to run towards the nautical end zone we'd created. He was fooling around, taking big steps and splashing, which was in keeping with our style of play to that point, when I saw Michael bearing down on Eli, faster than I would have thought possible, almost leaping across the water, making as little splash as he could, as if he were deliberately putting each foot in the water like a diver looking for the least resistance. Eli wasn't stocky by any description, but Michael was slim. Still, Michael tackled Eli like a linebacker in a football highlight reel, taking him down in the water, the ball squirting out of Eli's hands. It was an unexpected but a beautiful tackle nonetheless, and my brother Stephen and I began to cheer.

Eli and Michael seemed to be horsing around, splashing each other, and I was reminded of the splash fights in our backyard pool when I was a boy. My father, brother, and I would wade right up to each other like crazy dueling nineteenth-century men with dangerously highly developed senses of honour and stand stalwart, facing each other, splashing each other in the face.

But after about twenty seconds it was clear this was different. I could only see Michael. Eli was being held underwater, and he was beginning to drown. Stephen and I called out and rushed over, and between us we dragged Michael off Eli and lifted Eli out of the water. Eli doubled over and immediately threw up. He shuddered a few times and finally stood up. Michael was standing a few feet away, his arms crossed like a rebellious lifeguard. His eyes were unfocused. Eli didn't look at Michael, and when he recovered his breath and composure, he spoke to me. "I have to go."

But it was Michael who began walking up the beach. Without stopping or turning around, he said, "Sorry about that. I got a little carried away. I'm going to walk to town and catch a bus home." I wanted to run after him, tell him not to go, but something in the way he walked away made me hold back.

ELI

A week after our game at Allan's cottage, I saw Michael on Sherbrooke Street, across the road from the Roddick Gates, those few
slim strands of iron set in stone that separate the rest of Montreal
from the McGill Commons where boys and girls play Frisbee and
football, and sip coffee, study, and flirt. He was looking more slender
than usual. We stopped awkwardly, like acquaintances who weren't
quite sure where they knew each other from or why.

"I'm really sorry about last week," Michael said, barely able to
look at me. He was sorry, but there was something else in his manner,
as if he felt more embarrassed and personally let down by his
behaviour than actually sorry for what he'd done. But I took him
at his word.

I reached out my hand – he had extended his – and said, "No
need to apologize. I'm very sorry too. About Sophie." I felt I needed
to add that last part, but as soon as I said the words, I knew they
were a mistake. Michael's body actually contracted as if someone
had hit him, and he pulled back his hand just as it touched mine.

Michael was no longer looking away. He was studying me like
I was a specimen in a jar. "No need to say sorry to me. It's George
you owe an apology to." I could have said a lot of things to defend
myself at this point, but there was no point. So I said nothing and
let Michael turn away.

George had been Sophie's boyfriend from Windsor. As I stood
in the middle of the wide sidewalk on Sherbrooke, the crowd of
pedestrians flowing around us like a river around two jagged rocks,
Michael turned and said, loudly enough for everyone walking by

72

to hear, "You don't steal another guy's girlfriend," as if it were the most obvious thing in the world. "You just don't fucking do that." And then he disappeared into the crowd.

All I could think about was that everyone walking by would think I had stolen Michael's girlfriend. And in some strange time-warped, counterfactual, what-might-have-been, wishful kind of way, perhaps I had. Michael was angry with me for doing what he hadn't done out of loyalty to some non-existent, non-applicable chivalric code of honour, and he was doubly angry with himself for not doing it first.

MICHAEL

I arrived a little before seven. Eli had chosen McGill's Stephen Leacock Building for his literary debut. The building was a mausoleum, especially in late November in Montreal, and as far removed from the lightness of the Leacock persona as you could get. I hadn't expected a large crowd for a poetry reading, but even I was surprised by the heart-rending lack of turnout. Down below, near the front of the lecture hall, I could see Eli looking nervous. Beside him was Sophie. And sitting beside her was Professor Mitchell. [Professor Mitchell was Eli's first creative writing professor. He taught the class where Eli and Allan first met. I never heard Eli or anyone else say anything nice about him, and I won't be the first to offer a contrary opinion here.]

I felt almost embarrassed to be there. I could see Eli whispering to Mitchell and looking at his watch. Mitchell cleared his throat and commenced. Judging by the way he spoke, you could be forgiven for assuming he was addressing the Roman Forum or Shakespeare's Globe. "Good evening everyone," he began in his portentous way. "Thank you for being with us here tonight. This evening it is my very special pleasure to introduce to you a new voice in poetry: Eli Tredman. I've had the distinct pleasure over this past year to get to know Eli, and more importantly, to get to know his work. And, I must tell you, when I first came across Eli's poetry I felt a distinct tingle run up my spine. Many people write verse, some reasonably well, but Eli is that rare breed: a natural born poet. His poetry is honest and true and it recreates the world anew. It is, all in all, a welcome antidote to much of the bloodless, academic verse that is

74

being passed off as poetry today. But, ladies and gentlemen, let us allow Eli's poetry to speak for itself. Eli!"

Eli, bless his ambitious little soul, walked to the podium carrying his black notebook and cleared his throat nervously. (But, to be fair, is there any other way to clear your throat? And who could really blame him.) He began to read in that earnest, heartfelt way of his. To this day, I cannot remember anything that he read, but what I cannot get out of my mind was *how* he read. It was like listening to and watching his father. The same rhythms, cadences, tone, and inflections. How he paused at the end of each line. The way he pushed his dark hair back from his hazel eyes and looked up at the audience, as if reassuring himself they hadn't disappeared on him while he was looking down at the page. It was like watching the output of a human photocopy machine. It would have been an incredible performance if the resemblance had stopped there, but the problem was that the content was the same. It was obvious that Eli was hopelessly under the influence of the great poet who happened to be his father. By the end of the reading, I felt sorry for him in a way I had never felt sorry for anyone before, except for myself. At the end, there was enthusiastic, if sparse, applause, and Eli allowed himself a smile.

After it was over, Eli was selling copies of his book, and I use the term loosely, because it was more of a homemade chapbook than a book – twenty-odd pages printed on what appeared to be a poor excuse for a mimeograph machine – for five dollars. I was about to dig into my pocket and hand over my daily food budget, when Eli shyly handed me a copy. We hadn't spoken since our encounter on Sherbrooke Street a few weeks earlier, but that night we both knew we were floating together in a state of limbo. We were not quite friends again, but the potential was still alive. Eli invited me out for the obligatory post-reading beer, but I declined, pleading fatigue and the need to study. He looked relieved, and then they were gone, professor, would-be poet, girlfriend, all of them. I hurried back to my apartment and sat down in front of my word processor. I didn't move for two hours.

I am fortunate to have few regrets in my life. Aside from that day in the water at Allan's cottage, I've never come close to physically hurting anyone. [I still don't know what came over me that day. I know for sure I wouldn't have drowned Eli. It would have been out of character.] I've never committed adultery or broken anything valuable or made any life-altering mistakes. But writing that book review that night is one of my regrets. Still, sometime around 2 a.m. I placed my fingers on the keyboard and began to write. I had reached the conclusion that I had the obligation, the moral duty, and the responsibility to art and to Eli to save him from a life of delusion and write an honest, constructive review.

Since then, I've written and read too many book reviews to remember. I've seen many books never get reviewed. And I've come to the conclusion that if a reviewer thinks a book is terrible, then he should walk away from the review. Silence is the best criticism. Life's too short and the book review sections of newspapers too slim. If you can't say something nice, as someone's mother used to say, find another book to review. The law of literary Darwinism dictates there's enough indifference out there to kill most infant books coaxed out into the world without someone having to play murderer. Writing a negative review is like shooting an endangered species. But I was young and hadn't reached the level of wisdom I have today. So I went ahead and wrote my review.

Once I started writing, I couldn't stop. It came quickly, and an hour later I had my five hundred words. I revised, self-edited, and was done. Two days later I picked up a copy of *The McGill Daily*, flipped through the pages with the speed and anticipation that only a writer, desperate for proof of his existence, can understand, and found my review.

As any journalist knows, his responsibility ends with the article or the review. The headline, which is often the only part of the article that anyone reads, is the breathtaking responsibility of the copy editor, like a closer in baseball or a special teams player in football, someone with a particularly limited but coveted skill and power. In the case of the headline writer, they have a good general knowledge of history, literature, and pop culture, and an affinity for wordplay, puns, allusions, and brevity. In a way, headline writers are the poets of journalism. But writers are not without their influence. A careful writer can seed his or her story with a lead or image or quote that a good headline writer can't afford to miss. Although I shouldn't have been surprised, I nearly spilled my coffee in the Van Houtte where I was eating breakfast when I saw the headline: "No Son of Adam." And then a deadening sense of remorse settled in my belly as I began to read.

We can't all be Adam – not even when we are his son. Thirty years ago, a young McGill student by the name of Leonard Cohen donned a leather jacket, put pen to paper, and made professors and fellow students quiver with excitement. Today the tradition of supporting McGill would-be writers continues. Last night, Eli Tredman, son of Canadian great Adam Tredman, launched his poetry career with his first chapbook entitled, *A Glimpse of Sun*. A sparse crowd was in attendance.

Very quickly it became obvious that young Eli has talent, but what was more painfully obvious was that he is still labouring in the long shadow of his two-time Governor General Award-winning father. The broken syntax, the startling imagery, the unobtrusive metre would be powerful if it hadn't already been done. But Eli has potential. Anyone who can write the poem "Tea Steeps" can obviously craft an image and evoke a whole lifetime of anticipated devotion in just a few lines.

"Young Eli"? What the fuck was I thinking? (Not to mention the gratuitous "would-be" preceding "writers.") The few lines above about "Tea Steeps" are the only part of the review I'm not completely ashamed of, not just because I was offering pure, unconditional praise, but because I knew that Eli was writing about Sophie.

If Eli is able to free himself of his father's influence and overbearing example, and can focus on where his talent lies, in a quieter, more restrained poetry that stakes out a more nuanced position on the role of art, then he can become a poet in his own right.

Today, over twenty years later, I still cringe when I think about that review. The utter arrogance that's the prerogative of youth. But at the time, I thought I was doing the right thing, balancing my responsibility as a journalist with the responsibility of a friend. Yes, I still considered Eli to be a friend. I knew that what I was writing was harsh, but I thought that was what Eli needed – a well-meaning jolt of truth to set him on the right path.

I didn't go to class that day. I stayed in my apartment, ordered in cheap pizza and drank two beers – my absolute limit – and watched morning shows, soaps, sit-coms, and dramas from morning until midnight. I've often wished I'd just picked up the phone and called Eli to apologize. But, for whatever reason, I didn't. Psychology 101 would suggest my critical review was a way to get back at Eli for stealing Sophie. To be honest, the thought had occurred to me. But even then I'd already realized that Sophie had never been mine. It took my undeveloped undergraduate brain months to accept that I hadn't been writing about Eli. I had been writing about myself.

ALLAN

I recognized the metaphorical murder-suicide inherent in Michael's "review," even if he didn't, as soon as it appeared in print. And I couldn't miss his natural style. It was the same whether he was writing or speaking. Always analyzing, commenting, as if he were speaking in parentheses or inserting footnotes. And to give him credit, he was often witty – but also brutally honest. Without mercy, for himself or anyone else, Michael was always trying to get at what lay behind things. His Achilles heel? He always had to be right.

But my priority was Eli.

I didn't want to call him right away, because it would be obvious that I pitied him, and my father had taught me at an early age that pity is about the worst thing you can offer another human being. I did check in with Sophie to ask how he was doing – unnecessarily miserably in her opinion – but waited forty-eight hours before calling him. The phone seemed to ring forever. Finally Eli answered. I told him I would be there in twenty minutes, and thought we could go for a walk.

Silence for the longest time. And then a weak, "Okay," uttered in the tone of a man half frozen in the North Atlantic after the *Titanic* went down, who has just barely made up his mind to reach out for the lifesaver being thrown to him.

I drove across the other half of the Mountain, past Mount Royal Cemetery, and down to the edge of Outremont. Eli and Sophie were living in the Plateau at the time, at the top of a long flight of flimsy stairs. It was the same neighbourhood where Eli's father had lived when he was driving a bus, courting his future wife, and carving out a place for himself in the Canadian literary canon. I rang and rang again. It took forever for Eli to answer. When he arrived at the door, he was a man in mourning. Dark hair disheveled. Unshaven. Hazel eyes glazed. Dressed shabbily in black. I half expected to see a ritual rip in his shirt, but thankfully his clothing was intact. He seemed to be alone. I asked him where Sophie was.

Eli shrugged. "I think she's leaving me."

I laughed. "You might want to comb your hair and throw some water on your face."

He nodded in a robotic way and turned back into this apartment. Shoulders slumped. That's when I noticed a slight burning smell. When I asked him about it, he said it was nothing and continued walking away. I told him he should check his stove. He pretended to do as I said and then followed me to the car doing his best zombie walk imitation. I placed the key in the ignition but before I started the car, I asked him again about the burning smell.

He didn't look at me but this time he replied. "I was burning my poems. All of them." Said as if he had been taking out the garbage.

"Who the fuck do you think you are?" I asked, laughing again. "Kafka?"

His reply? "How do you even know who Kafka is?"

"I hoped you at least saved copies." Maybe he wasn't Kafka, but Eli was good. The thought crossed my mind that I was about to try to take advantage of his youthful disappointment. But I reminded myself I was going to offer him something valuable in return. I had always liked to drive fast, even in the city, but I drove slowly that day in deference to Eli's mood. As I drove back towards the Mountain, he asked where we were going.

"I thought we'd take a walk on the Mountain. Park at Beaver Lake and head up to the lookout." I tried to sound upbeat but not too cheery. There's nothing worse for a depressed person than to be confronted by someone who can't find fault in anything and who wants nothing more than to be grateful for being born into God's world.

"Sounds pretty symbolic to me."

Ten minutes later we parked at Beaver Lake and started to make our way along the path that winds its way up to the summit and the lookout. I don't remember what we talked about for most of the walk. I assume books, movies, school. Anything but the reason why we were there. It was only when we reached the lookout and stopped at the edge of the concrete balustrade that I worked up the courage to broach the topic. The city was stretched out below us, and it was quiet where we were, the traffic a distant murmur.

"How are you feeling?" I couldn't believe it as soon as the words were out of my mouth. It sounded like something a psychiatrist would say.

"I'm embarrassed."

"What did your father say?"

"He said it was the most ridiculous review he'd read. He told me I should write a letter to the editor fighting back. Something like Byron's *English Bards and Scotch Reviewers*."

"Are you going to do it?"

Eli shook his head. "I'm not my father."

"You know, you don't have to respond to a negative review the same way he would have."

"No, I mean I'm *not* my father."

I was silent for a moment, because that seemed like the right thing to do. "Eli," I said, and at that point I think I did something a good friend is supposed to do — at least they always do so in the movies. I grabbed his shoulder in a supportive way and said, "Look, you know I barely know a thing about poetry, even after enduring Mitchell and hanging out with you." Yes, I could come up with the ideas but someone else had to put them down on paper. And my father always taught me that if people are going to want to help you, they first have to believe they are better than you. "But I know

81

two things: one, you are a good poet and you still have a lot of time to prove it. And two, you are too good a poet and too good a person to be wasting your time worrying about reviews.

"In politics, you have to come to terms with the fact that not everybody is going to love you, or you get the fuck out of the way. You've always got thirty per cent who will support you no matter what you do, who will vote for you because their parents and grandparents have always voted for your party, or because they hate the other party, or because they have a world view that never changes. You've got another thirty per cent who hate you for the same reasons, and will never vote for you no matter what you do or who you are – you could be Jesus Christ for all they care. Then you've got another thirty per cent who are looking for a reason to make up their mind. Those are the only ones you worry about." And I looked out at the city for a minute or so, building up the suspense. "If you look down below, what do you see?" I asked.

"The city?"

"Yeah. If you look over there you see my father's riding." I pointed it out for Eli, who still really knew nothing about politics. "It's over there. We're going to graduate in the spring and there's going to be an election in the fall, and my father's decided not to run. He's going to retire and spend some time with my mother. I think they call it catching up. I've been thinking about this for a long time, ever since the day after you helped me win the student election. I'm going to run for Parliament." Eli looked at me. He had an unreadable expression on his face, but I thought at the time he was just impressed. I was so full of myself at that point that I didn't realize how bad my timing was. I went on without thinking.

"The student election was the dress rehearsal for this, but I see a seat in Parliament as just the beginning of a long journey that could end…." I left a very pregnant pause and didn't fill in the blank. "Anyway, it's going to be a long journey not without hardship and challenge. I don't know exactly what it holds in store, but I know one thing."

At this point, Eli was supposed to say, "And what is that?" but it was one of his most charming qualities that he only said what he had to and never exactly what he was supposed to. He just looked at me, so I went on: "I know I'll need someone like you."

At this point, Eli laughed. I was a bit taken aback, but glad to see him finally relaxed enough to laugh out loud.

"Someone like me?" said incredulously, as if he were the most useless member of society. I already knew that was the not-so-secret, largely un-confessed, unacknowledged fear of most poets, and the source of their singular arrogance about their vocation. That beneath their ability to juggle words like a circus performer, they felt they were really a sham, outsiders with no purpose, completely at odds with the world of goods and business and practical concerns, charlatans who puffed themselves up with inflated claims of influence because they had none to speak of.

"Yeah. When you cut right through it all, politics is about vision, which is a fancy word for communications. I want you to come with me and grow into the role, like I will grow into mine. Right now we are two puppies, tripping over our ambitious feet. What does that Shelley guy say again, something about poets being the unacknowledged legislators of the world? Sounds a bit like wishful thinking to me, but I am offering you the chance to be an acknowledged legislator, or," and I turned on the charm, "at least help one directly. And, if we both fail," and here I smiled, so he understood my next words were meant in the right spirit, "at least you will have something to write about other than what you read about or hear in your courses."

He laughed again, as if I were the most amusing person in the world. "I write bad poetry. I wrote a couple of speeches for you and came up with a few sound bites. What are you thinking?"

All I told Eli by way of preparation was that my father was different. I wasn't sure if this would be much use to him. Perhaps it was unfair of me not to tell him more, but it would have been a double disservice to me and to him if I had overly prepared him. One Friday night I invited Eli over for supper. My mother was out for the evening at a Montreal Children's Hospital Foundation board meeting, so it was just me, my father, Eli, and the cook.

Conversation, as always with my father, started easily enough. My father was always excessively polite, almost to the point of obsession. I had never heard him ask for something without saying "Please," and had never seen him accept anything without a sincere "Thank you." He had the most beautiful manners I ever saw in another human being. He always spoke in a low voice, every word chosen carefully to convey his exact meaning. I never saw him raise his voice, either at home or in Parliament. He was one of those rare people in the late twentieth century who spoke in complete sentences, and he never misspoke or had to start over. He always dressed formally, even on weekends, when he might take the liberty of wearing a suit without a tie. He never drank or swore that I knew of, and his nickname among his political colleagues was "The Bishop," which he took as a compliment in that polite way of his, a half-smile playing out across his face.

Whenever he was meeting someone for the first time, his only objective was to put them at ease, and this he did within minutes of shaking Eli's hand – firmly but not so firmly that it felt like physical intimidation. My father learned early on, or perhaps knew instinctively, that most people like to hear and talk about themselves, and he had a disarming way of being genuinely interested in other people. If you weren't on your toes or naturally suspicious, you wouldn't realize you were being subjected to the most skilful and subtle interrogation, designed to elicit the maximum information about your character, your motives, your values. For those who knew this, like Eli, the experience of having one of Canada's most successful ministers of finance ever express a personal interest in you was not unpleasant, and so you went along, and it was like taking a comforting drug, or like lying on the beach in warm shallow water and letting a gentle surf flow over you.

After about half an hour of this, my father glanced over at me, so quickly that Eli probably didn't notice, engrossed as he was in talking about literature and poetry and the role of art in civic life. To most people it would have seemed an innocent, fatherly glance, a check-in over dinner to see how his oldest son was doing while he spoke to his friend about university, but to me it was a gently reproving glance, and I knew why. My father was too polite to say anything and too sophisticated ever to bully me or any of my friends, but I'd been listening to the conversation between him and Eli, and over the course of twenty odd minutes, my father had proven without a doubt that Eli didn't have the right kind or level of experience to run communications for an aspiring rookie MP from Montreal who also, and most importantly, happened to be his son.

In the course of the unofficial job interview, Eli had revealed – no, that is the wrong word, he didn't even have the sense to think about concealing – the fact that his lifetime political communications experience consisted of running one campaign for student government which had come within eleven votes of being unsuccessful. He had written four speeches, two of which I had used, and had prepared his candidate for a grand total of three interviews, all with the student newspaper. My father was a reasonable man, and he understood that everybody had to start somewhere. Just not with his son.

I was about to jump into the middle of the inquisition and defend Eli, defend the potential that I knew was there beneath the insecure undergrad, the talent that was waiting to be discovered, and if I had, everything would have turned out differently, because everything would have been lost. My father would never have had the confidence in him. But as I was about to make a mistake, and actually, as I had already started to speak, Eli politely cut me off and began the self-rescue mission.

"Minister Keyes, I very much appreciate the time you are taking to meet with me tonight, and I just want to say a few words. I recognize your son is about to begin his political career, and the importance of that, and I know that what we did together at McGill doesn't even rise to the level of a rehearsal. I recognize Allan is about to begin the real race, and that there is no allowance for any missteps. I also am aware that I don't have twenty years experience. I haven't run communications for Cabinet ministers or premiers. Your son would be taking a risk on me. But I want to assure you that it would be a calculated risk. First of all, I believe in Allan. When I helped him with his student council campaign it was obvious to anyone who heard or saw him that he has a gift. He knows what people want and what they need. People listen to him when he speaks. He says things that people want to listen to. I can help him say those things.

"I know you think I am young, but I will work twice as hard as someone who has been doing this for twenty years, and I will be doubly careful about not making mistakes. And I learn quickly. Because I don't have the experience, I will have to work harder and think harder. But I'm confident I will end up reaching the right conclusions.

"I'm not an arrogant person. Everybody has an ego, sure, and I make up my own mind, but I'm not afraid to take advice. I'm not afraid to admit that I don't know everything. I listen to people, just as I listened to you tonight as you were asking me questions and trying to make up your mind about me. If you have someone who helps you with your communications, or just someone who you think is the best in the field, I would be more than happy to consult them as I go.

"Perhaps most importantly, I have integrity. I'm always going to give Allan the best benefit of my professional advice, without regard to what I think he might want to hear, or to what is popular, or to what even he wants to do. I will tell him what is right, both from a pragmatic and from an ethical point of view. My biggest motivation is to do the right thing and do a good job.

"I recognize the significance of what Allan is setting out on. I would never, ever put myself or Allan in a position where I felt he was at risk. If I thought that was the case, I would not be here tonight. I would have told Allan that I could not serve with him. If you have made up your mind about me, I understand, but if you believe that I might be able to help Allan, I would be very happy to tell you what he and I have in mind for his first campaign."

My father looked at Eli for an uncomfortably long time, and Eli didn't fidget or speak once during that period. He just sat there patiently, appearing calm even though I could only imagine what was going on in his head, and he was respectful of my father and his intrusive silence. He was exhibiting three of my father's most prized virtues, plus the *sine qua non*, honesty, or as my father politely put it, an innate inability to bend the truth, all bundled into one twenty-one-year old, inexperienced, more than slightly insecure package. After our conversation on the Mountain, Eli had acquitted himself well on the first step of his quest to write words that would change people's lives. My father glanced at me again, and turned back to Eli. "Tell me what you're thinking." Eli was halfway in.

PART II

Ottawa

ELI

Every hero needs a dragon. Without a fire-breathing, murderous, flying, mythical beast with a taste for human flesh to slay, you can never inspire a poem, win the king's daughter, or earn the kingdom. Like all heroes, Allan knew this at an early age. You would think he had no fear, the way he would water-ski on Lake Memphremagog, or race his BMW down the highway to the Townships at 160 km an hour, the radar detector rattling on the dashboard, or drink late into the night and early morning until he could barely stand. But as you got to know him, you came to understand he had enough fear in him – he was just good at hiding it behind unblinking blue eyes, steady hands, and a self-deprecating sense of humour that never let him down, whether behind the podium in front of a thousand people, on TV in front of millions, or at the neighbourhood Tim Hortons.

His humour was one of his secret weapons, and I sometimes think it helped him win more than one election. It's become a bit of a truism, at least in North America – where we want our leaders to be as much like us as possible – that we vote for the candidate we would most like to sit down and have a beer with. The truth is we vote for the candidate who is most comfortable with himself. And that often turns out to be the candidate who appears not to take himself too seriously.

At some point, long before I had met him, Allan had learned to tame his fear, not by ignoring or enduring it, as most people learn to cope with fear, but by going out and looking for it. One late afternoon after we had both finished our classes for the day,

91

we were walking to his car when we saw a cat chasing a mouse along the sidewalk. The cat was a big, long-limbed tabby, white with gray stripes and scarred ears, and it was gaining on the mouse. It reminded me of Art Spiegelman's graphic novel about the Holocaust, where he draws the Nazis as cats and the Jews as mice. As this mouse turned from the sidewalk into an alley, the cat tensed to make its final pounce. Then the mouse, as if realizing everything was lost unless it did something completely out of the ordinary to change the rules and the inescapable ending, suddenly stopped and turned around to face the cat. In what seemed like a special effects scene in a movie, the mouse actually began to run directly toward the cat. The cat – surprised, stunned, bewildered – did a double take and turned tail. Minutes later, as we stepped into Allan's car and he was about to turn on the ignition, he turned to me: "You saw that mouse back there?"

"Yeah?"

"That's me. That's how I live my life." He wasn't being funny or ironic, or boasting in any way. He wasn't trying to convince me that was really the way it was. It's just how he saw himself. Stopping always to confront his fear, and chase it down or chase it away.

My own fear at the time was simple: I was afraid of failing Allan, of letting him down because of my inexperience, of helping to destroy his career before it had a chance to begin. I was afraid of my youth, my short history on this planet, my lack of street smarts, my poor sense of how things actually worked in the real world outside of books. Because of all this, I was unsure of my ability to come up with the right words for him. When you are young and afraid of things like this, you tend to make one of two mistakes: you either listen too much to other people or you don't listen enough. One of the hardest things in life is to take a lot of advice and then make up your own mind about the right thing to do. You have to sift through everyone's agendas, their different ways of looking at their world, and then discount or value their various experiences that cause them to make certain judgments.

When you are young, everyone assumes you lack experience, and by and large you do, but after working for over twenty years, I've found that experience can be a double-edged sword. It can make you complacent, lazy even. You stop thinking, relying only on instincts formed from having seen various patterns over and over again, knowing how each has played out before. What I didn't realize at the time, when I was starting out with Allan, was that I had one quality that helped make up for my lack of almost everything else. It's the quality I seek when I'm looking to hire in the PMO. I don't tend to get seduced by long years in service, by the war stories that every long-serving flack can tell, the stories of all the famous people they've met and had drinks with. I look for judgment. True judgment is often formed by experience, but more often I've found it's innate. You can improve upon it, or let it atrophy, but you're either born with good judgment or you're not.

Allan's father wanted his son to run in the safest riding in Montreal: his own. Allan's father's former advisers, who had ill-defined but still powerful roles in our campaign – this was the compromise under which Allan's father had agreed that I would run communications for his son – held the same opinion. It would have been easy. The name recognition alone would have probably won it for Allan. But Allan and I both refused. We made a judgment call, and we stuck up for ourselves. We knew that Allan could reduce the risk of losing to almost nothing this way, but for the rest of his career he would be seen as the man who had walked, if not been carried into, his father's seat. And most importantly, Allan and I wouldn't have learned the things we both knew we needed to learn. So we picked a riding far removed from Westmount. Rosemont – La Petite-Patrie had been held for nearly twenty years by one of the longest-serving Cabinet ministers in the current government. Everyone expected Allan to get his comeuppance, to lose and lose badly. And that was exactly where we wanted to be: in the absolute dungeon of expectations.

We started off, not with a grand vision, but with the most basic retail politics. We knew that people had to feel comfortable with Allan before they would let themselves be inspired by him. Allan happily accepted every offer to speak in every church basement, every community hall, every billiard hall, every *casse-croute*, every tavern, every nursing home. He abandoned English for French and Italian, and he spoke both languages like a native speaker, not just at ease among the words and idiomatic expressions, and not just with the right accent, but with the appropriate gestures and facial expressions, the right way of looking at and responding to the world. He shook hands like a Walmart greeter on speed, kissed babies like he was their mother, embraced unwashed drunks like they were his long-lost brothers. He appeared on every local talk show and appeared twice on MusiquePlus, the new French music video channel, where his youth, fashion sense, and spontaneously planned *a capella* rendition of a local pop song locked up the local youth vote in less than half an hour.

Allan hated doughnuts – he thought they were too sweet and felt they made him fat – but he spent some of his best campaigning and listening hours in Dunkin' Donuts shops, and he learned to eat our country's holy food, lots of them, and to drink regular coffee with generous helpings of milk and sugar. After a while he began to enjoy them and compensated with an extra workout here and there. A change in clothes went hand in hand with a change in eating habits. Allan preferred well-tailored suits, cut in the narrower European style – Boss and Zegna in particular – and even in university, when everyone else was wearing jeans and polo shirts, he liked to dress up. But when he was running for MP he put his good suits away – he kept them for trips to Europe – and had five suits custom-made to look more North American, a bit boxier, more baggy, and ill-fitting. A good politician must be a bit of a chameleon, ready to change his skin when he crawls onto a different branch.

We opened up a small, welcoming office beside a corner store on Sherbrooke, and hired Louise Lachance, the tenth daughter in a family of fifteen, mother of five, and a young grand-mère of three at the age of forty-five, as our receptionist. She had worked her whole life as a receptionist in small local businesses but was between jobs. Louise knew everyone in the neighbourhood. Sometimes I thought she was related to everyone in the neighbourhood. Other times I thought she was responsible for getting out more than half our vote.

We stayed at the office every night until 11 p.m., hunched over our desks, working the phones, meeting with constituents and voters. I've always been amazed that it doesn't matter how early you start work in the morning – it could be 4 a.m. – but if you leave by 5 p.m., you're considered a clock puncher. However, if you don't leave work until after supper, you could start at noon, and you would still have a reputation as a hard worker. Allan started early as well, but we also took advantage of the perceptions that are accorded to those who stay late.

Every weekend, Allan played charity rugby games to raise money for some cause or another that meant something to the local neighbourhoods, and we became involved in efforts to raise adult literacy rates. One night, Allan was tackled in a scrum and broke his shoulder. The next day he was doped up, with his arm in his sling, speaking to a local service group, gaining sympathy and applause from men who didn't give either freely. I used to tease Allan that the main motivation for university rugby players was not to actually play but to get injured and impress women in bars with their bruises and bandages and casts. Allan laughed and didn't bother to deny it.

Another time, with under a week to go before the election,

a seven-foot-tall giant, who was a volunteer for Allan's opponent, head-butted Allan in a scrum, and Allan was badly cut above his right eye. Allan's father had been playing a weekly game of squash for twenty years with Montreal's best plastic surgeon, and Allan could have been fixed up better than before, but he decided to let his forehead heal, and scar, on its own. And in between getting injured, Allan was speaking and taking questions, and expressing empathy, and kissing babies, and shaking hands, and hugging drunks and grandmothers all day and late into the night while his opponent was buried in reports and committees and working hard behind a desk in Ottawa to keep the country running.

In every speech, Allan articulated his passion for Rosemont – La Petite-Patrie: its people, its challenges, its tenements of factory workers, its unemployed, its hungry children, its high school dropouts who filled the minimum wage jobs, and its senior citizens who had to make decisions about whether to buy food or turn the heat on in the winter. He promised to stand up for them in Ottawa. And in every speech Allan thundered against the incumbent for being out of touch, for having grown too big for the riding, for being too aloof, for being stuck in the past. And in the end, when all the ballots were in and all the votes were counted, and after we waited for the results among our supporters down in one of the local taverns, Allan won. He won because he worked hard, because people liked and trusted him. He won because he was young and energetic, and because people were flattered that one of Westmount's chosen sons had descended from Montreal's mountain to their concrete plains to seek their votes and support. And he won because, unlike his intelligent, accomplished, powerful but old-fashioned and buttoned-down opponent, he looked good on TV and was as good with words as he was on the playing field.

Allan won, and I became a minor league communications sensation, at least in Montreal and in very narrow political circles. Other communications people in the Party and the occasional politician began to come calling to seek my advice on one issue or another. And it was around this time that I began to go grey. I started off with a little around the temples, just flecks really. After about a year, I started to be a little more fearless with the dye, and the grey became noticeable. Five years later, when I turned twenty-six, it was taken for granted. Sophie used to laugh at me for what she saw as reverse if not perverse vanity, but it accomplished its purpose.

With Allan's win, and my greying hair, Allan's father's former advisers started to look at me a little differently when I walked into a room. They didn't always ask me to explain my reasoning from beginning to end. They took more of my analysis and conclusions for granted. The wise old men of the Party – you have to remember this was nearly two decades before youth seemed to become the prime qualification for electoral success – began to make a little more time for me at cocktail parties and policy and strategy planning retreats. With this success – which was based on words, but which I owed to myself and not in any way to my father – my early trans-formation was complete. And so I grew early into middle age and easy perceptions of capability and experience.

MICHAEL

After I graduated, I decided I wanted to leave Montreal. I moved to Ottawa to freelance and, after a couple of years, I got a job as a reporter covering national politics with the *Ottawa Citizen*. (I would use the *Citizen* as my springboard to land a full-time gig covering politics at *The Mail and Post* five years later.) I had been born several decades too late to be living in the Golden Age of print journalism – we had to contend with TV and radio – but there was no Twitter or Internet or bloggers yet. [The Internet as we know it was spawned in the early nineties and the first-ever infernal tweet was sent internally on March 21, 2006. I even remember attending an exceptionally dull seminar on how to use the Internet offered by the Ottawa Public Library in 1995.] Print journalists, with our stories and bylines and daily deadlines, were still taken seriously and read carefully. It didn't hurt that every second person in Ottawa seemed to work for the government and everyone looked intelligent.

Leaving Montreal was partly to escape Eli and partly to escape Sophie – even though I had to admit to myself I had hardly even known her – but it was mainly to escape Quebec's language laws that were entering their second decade of existence. Although I had taken late French immersion in junior high, I knew early on that I was never going to earn my living stringing words together for *La Presse* or *Le Devoir*. And writing for a dwindling linguistic minority never held much attraction.

When Allan was first elected, Eli started spending a lot of time in our capital city. Despite the fact we were no longer friends, I couldn't help seeing him on the Hill or at Hy's or in the ByWard Market on Thursday or Friday nights or on the weekend. [Hy's is a well-known steakhouse in downtown Ottawa and a popular hangout for lobbyists, politicos, and journalists. It's where people went, and still go, to be seen. I cannot tell you how many scoops were served up to me there over the years, among the steaks and martinis.] When we ran into each other I wouldn't mention and he wouldn't bring up the review or the incident in the water. Or Sophie. Instead we would exchange pleasantries, harmless political gossip, and I would sometimes call him to ask for an interview with Allan, which he would sometimes grant. And I couldn't help following his career.

I never told him this, and I admit it sounds harsh, but in the first year of his career, Eli sucked at what he did. He hung on, I assume, mostly because Allan for some reason liked him. (But maybe, as I think about it, "sucked" is too strong a word, and applicable only in comparison to how excellent Eli became later on.) I also never told Eli why he was not very good when he started off, because that would have been at best embarrassing, and at worst, a betrayal of my journalistic profession.

Eli began with all the best motives, with faith and confidence in media relations and public communications. It was the same Boy Scout faith he used to bring to his poems, before he exchanged the politics of poetry for the poetry of politics. But like a man who didn't yet know how to swim and who'd been dropped into a big, wide, fast-moving river, he feared but didn't really understand the medium. He spoke in long, complex sentences with qualifiers, bracketed thoughts, and subordinate clauses that competed for position – and which made it easy for us journalists to cut and splice what we wanted. His naturally formal language, which surprisingly was not as bad in person as it was on the page, was still on full display.

When communicating policy, he earnestly lectured us, like a geologist explaining the complex effects of the passage of time on precious stone formations, instead of presenting himself as a discreet and trusted diamond cutter, offering us small irresistible jewels, polished versions of the truth. He was a verbal novelist rather than the practitioner of haiku that he needed to be. He didn't deliberately ignore Cyril Connolly's smack-down that "Literature is the art of writing something that will be read twice; journalism what will be grasped at once," because he'd probably never read it once, let alone twice.

He didn't distinguish between the different media, didn't ensure his language was precise and perfect when he was speaking to a print reporter, that he was cool and sunny when he was on TV, energetic on radio. He didn't know that if he was doing a taped TV or radio interview and he flubbed a line he could ask for a re-take and the reporter would oblige (unless maybe you had stolen his girlfriend). He got nervous when he was doing live interviews, missing an opportunity because he didn't realize he was completely in control of his unedited message.

In the beginning he returned every phone call and answered every question, no matter how unrelated to his message. Even worse for him, he always answered the phone. He accepted every request to do an interview. He was overly polite, but he was sloppy in the technical department. When he provided an answer, and the reporter didn't immediately proceed to the next question, letting the question hang there in the air, Eli was uncomfortable. He felt compelled to fill the silence and ended up volunteering additional information, going down roads he shouldn't. He was too anxious to please, when he should have just sat tight with his concise original answer and smiled, waiting out the reporter, waiting for the next question. He was embarrassed about giving non-answers to genuine questions, hesitant to reframe the questions in the way he would have liked to answer them. He was reluctant to imply that he hoped the reporters had their questions ready for his answers, as Trudeau so stylishly quipped at the opening of a press conference.

He desperately wanted to be liked.

He didn't get when he should have been putting Allan in front of the cameras – when he had some big good news – and when he himself should have been running interference, being boring, handling the run-of-the-mill or the inconvenient questions. When he spoke, he gave the impression he had memorized his talking points like an ambitious undergrad presenting in front of his class, and if you threw a question at him in a sequence that differed from the one he had prepared for, he was rattled.

He didn't know where his responsibilities ended and ours began. When Allan gave a speech, and we reported on what Eli considered to be minor aspects of the message, he called us to convince us we had missed the main point. When we covered a story and quoted the PM at the beginning of the story, analyzed his arguments in the middle, and left Allan's Leader-of the-Opposition reaction for the final paragraphs that most readers wouldn't ever read, Eli phoned to tell us we were biased and not giving each side of the argument equal weight. Eli didn't yet realize that when he had to call us after the fact to explain or complain, he hadn't done his job. It was his fault, not ours.

He didn't know anything about politics, economics, or the way the world worked. He didn't have the political jargon or the obligatory pretence of credibility down pat. He didn't yet know how to fake it. Most of all, he didn't recognize the place that the media interview occupied in the hierarchy of communications. As every good general knows, the battle isn't won on the battlefield, in the fog of war, in the midst of the misunderstood orders, or under the pressure of time. It's won long before any of that. Eli assumed he could simply ready himself or Allan and then do the interview, and all would be well. He was overly confident in words and his ability to use them, in the soundness of his logic, the strength of his arguments. He hadn't begun to think about how to prepare the public for the message or work with the context of his environment, didn't yet get the value of going out and talking to people directly without the filter of the medium. He didn't yet know that media relations was just the tip of the iceberg, that actions always speak louder than words. Words always trail far behind, bringing up the rear, mopping up after the real work is done. It's always what you do that counts the most.

ELI

Sophie and I spent our honeymoon in Quebec City, at the Château Frontenac, back when we had no money and thought we had no time. We were both starting our careers, working long days and every weekend, I at Allan's side and she as an editor for the educational publisher Rawdon & Sons. We gave ourselves three days and two nights and made the three-hour drive from Montreal to Quebec City right after the wedding reception. We had been married on neutral ground, or, more appropriately, in No Man's Land, at the McGill Chapel. Although neither of us was very observant, we wanted to have a ceremony that was both Christian and Jewish, and our hope was to have a rabbi officiate. But no rabbi agreed to marry us unless Sophie agreed to convert or we promised to raise the children as Jewish.

I found out later that other couples in the same predicament made the promise and then did whatever they wanted, but we didn't feel comfortable about that, so we found a willing minister from the United Church who had grey hair and kind eyes and who gladly talked about Jesus and Jehovah in equal measure, and who agreed to the breaking of the wine glass and reading of the psalms. One of Sophie's friends read a sonnet, we exchanged rings and vows, and I stomped firmly on the glass, crushing it into shards in the heavy white linen napkin, reminding myself with my quick action of the fragility of relationships, where one thoughtless moment can have irrevocable and everlasting consequences. And no, Michael was not there. When we were drawing up the invitation list, Sophie had suggested that I add his name. But aside from scrumming on the Hill, speaking professionally over the phone, or making what passed for conversation when we saw each other on the streets or in the bars of Ottawa, we hadn't really spoken for over five years. Ever since I had "stolen" Sophie, Michael had literally tried to drown me, and then tried to drown me in print. As we planned the wedding, Sophie asked me so many times whether I was inviting Michael that I started to worry maybe she had a secret crush on him. In the end I relented, but by the time I mailed out the invitation our wedding was two weeks away. We never received a reply.

Following the ceremony, we held our reception at the Mount Stephen Club, where neither Sophie nor I had ever set foot, but where Allan had a membership. I don't recall much about the reception, although I'm sure we had good food and good wine and the guests enjoyed themselves, but I do remember my father read a poem and Allan gave a toast. My father read one of his own poems, of course, one he had composed for the occasion. He stood up in his dark blue pinstriped suit – the only one he owned – and his Birkenstocks, without socks. Like any poem written with a purpose or for an occasion, and like the work of any poet laureate no matter how good they are before they accept that ceremonial kiss of death, it sounded a little forced, less like a poem and more like a highbrow homework assignment. It was heartfelt and true but perhaps coincidentally, or perhaps because of that, it wasn't one of my father's better works. Too many words and not enough tension, the sincerity getting in the way of the art. Despite all that, it meant a lot to Sophie, and after the wedding she had the words done up in calligraphy on good paper and framed, and hung it in our dining room above our antique buffet table. Despite the fact my father wrote the words and that I must have stared at them thousands of times while eating dinner, I have trouble remembering his poem, but I somehow can't forget Allan's toast.

At some point in the evening Allan stood up, raised his glass, and the room quieted, as if everybody had been watching and waiting for him to speak at just that moment. His fiancée Katherine was sitting beside him, and her unbroken gaze directed up at him as he began to speak was like a spotlight. Allan and Katherine wouldn't marry for another two years, but they already acted as if they had been husband and wife for decades. Sophie and I had observed this on more than one occasion with a measure of innocuous envy. The two of them seemed to already know everything there was to know about themselves and each other, and they were comfortable with it all. Like some married couples, they shared a strong resemblance. They were both tall and blond and self-deprecating.

Katherine had grown up two streets over from Allan in Westmount, and they had seen each other often at the same teenage parties. She left Montreal to attend Yale, where she graduated *summa cum laude* with a major in economics and a minor in drama. After she returned to Montreal, the two of them had met up again in Westmount Park after one of Allan's rugby games. Although this fact never appeared in any media story, Katherine was already by this time and would remain one of Allan's key political advisers. She would become the main architect of our Party's economic policy and would draft the economic platform for the election in which Allan would be elected PM. Allan and I were pleased when Sophie and Katherine hadn't just tolerated each other – as friends' spouses often do – but had become real friends.

Allan was smiling like a king at the wedding of his closest courtier, relishing the outpouring of goodwill, willing into being with the purity of his words a lifetime of love between two people he cared about. "Tonight it brings me great pleasure to toast the marriage of two people who are special to all of us and very special to me: Eli and Sophie. If you are a reader of books, as Eli is, then you know that Dante had his Beatrice, Petrarch his Laura, Tristan his Isolde, and Romeo his Juliet. If you are a lover of life then you know that our Eli has his Sophie. And I can say with the highest authority, having spent many, many days with both Eli and Sophie, that they could teach a thing or two to all those lovers we read about in books.

"Sophie is blessed with Eli, for in Eli she is marrying a man who is not only humble and down to earth, empathetic and gifted with words, but also devoted and faithful and loyal. Anyone who is lucky enough to count Eli as a friend knows he will always be there for you, no matter how dark the night or high the mountain. Eli is the kind of person they tell stories about, the kind of man who would throw himself on a grenade without a second's thought to save those he holds dear. Eli is also a man without a false bone in his body, a man who couldn't lie if his life depended on it, a man who is not afraid to speak the truth. In fact, he is a man who is compelled to speak the truth without thought of what his listener might want to hear, or what might be good for his career. I know this from first-hand experience." Laughter. "He is a very special person."

"And in Sophie, Eli is doubly blessed, for Sophie was meant for Eli. Sophie is a person with a big heart, a person who cares not only about Eli, but about her friends, her family, and every stray animal who is fortunate enough to cross her path. I cannot tell you how many times I have seen Sophie take in a stray cat or crow, or even a mouse, to nurse back to health. Sophie wears her intelligence and her talent and her beauty lightly, without affectation, without arrogance. When I see Eli and Sophie together, holding hands or talking softly or just sitting in silence, I am reminded of Plato's idea of love, and I believe that Eli and Sophie were once one soul that was split apart at birth into two halves and now they have been reunited and are one again. Please join me in a toast to many, many years of love and happiness for both of them, our dearest friends." And everyone applauded because Allan's words rang eloquently and true for them, and everyone drank deeply.

On our honeymoon, we did the usual things, like walk for hours in the Old Town, eat and drink in centuries-old stone houses that had been reborn as gourmet restaurants, visit the Musée national des beaux-arts, climb the stairs to the Plains of Abraham where over two hundred years earlier a few men in red coats charged a rock bluff and changed history, and took a boat cruise on the St. Lawrence. And, in what became a tradition without us ever planning it, each year to mark our anniversary we returned like homing pigeons to spend a night in the castle-like hotel guarding the Old Town.

I can't remember what the call that woke me up was about – probably some emergency that seemed important at the time but which a year or even a month later you can't even recall – but one night, on our second anniversary trip to Quebec City, my phone started vibrating on my bedside table at 2 a.m. I answered, but before starting to speak I put on a shirt and pants and took the call outside in the hallway so as not to wake Sophie. I like to walk around when I'm on my cell phone. I must have walked halfway down one of the Château's long hallways when up ahead a man left a room. He looked like a university student, young and disheveled, as if he'd been awake forever. By the time he reached the elevator, I had turned around and was walking back the way I had come.

I must have walked up and down that hallway five or six more times, bringing order to chaos, offering my wisdom, solving some intractable problem that required my attention in the middle of the night. Twenty minutes later I was at the other end of the hallway when I saw another man leave a room. If I hadn't been pacing up and down the hotel hallway in the middle of the night like Albert Speer marching across the world in his Spandau cell, if I hadn't been facing towards his room when he emerged, if he hadn't stopped when he saw me and faltered for a split second like a man watching his life unravel, and if I hadn't seen the look of pure animal fear on his pale face, like an innocent deer blundering onto a highway,

I probably never would have realized that he'd come out of the same room as the other man. As he walked by me, he couldn't look me in the eye, and almost hid his face, like a man on trial coming out of the courtroom in handcuffs, turning away from the camera.

When I returned to my room, I slowly undressed and got back into bed beside Sophie, careful not to waken her. I pulled the blankets up high, lay on my back, and stayed awake for hours, unsure about what to do with what I had just seen. In the morning I settled on doing nothing. At least for the time being. It would be years before I could take advantage of that seemingly small decision.

Nine months after our anniversary in Quebec City, Sophie was in the delivery room. After a prolonged labour that started off slowly, everything happened quickly. Sophie was sweating and in pain, having decided, and having held to her decision, to have a natural birth. The greatest hits opera CD that she loved and that I gave her for her last birthday was playing loudly on the portable stereo I brought in with our overnight bags. I was rubbing her back like some crazed Rasputin-like masseur, and talking motivation into her ear. She was not really understanding or even hearing the words, but my voice soothed her. The nurse was screaming, "Push, Push," like a lusty rowing coach, followed by "Breathe, Breathe," and the doctor on duty, who was soft-spoken and gentle with small, delicate hands, cradled the baby's head, which was crowning now. It was dark and wet and slimy, and it was like watching the movie *Alien,* where the creature from outer space bursts screaming out of some-one's unsuspecting belly.

My first son was born with the cord around his neck. He came out blue, looking like a miniature Dracula. His fingers were long and greyish, and his fingernails were blood red. And he came out silent and limp. He didn't cry as babies do in the movies. I'd never seen a baby being born in real life, but I'd seen it so many times on the screen that my brain had been tricked into assuming I knew exactly what it was like.

For the first few minutes I thought he was dead. Sophie was exhausted. She looked at me and asked if everything was okay. I felt pale and dizzy, the room was too warm, and I nodded, yes, yes. I went over to the head of the bed, held her hand and squeezed it. The nurses went to work on our baby and brought him around. Later I learned about Apgar scores and that our son's was barely above the level it would have been if he were dead. I worried about oxygen deprivation, birth defects, the mental handicap he would have to carry around with him for a lifetime because of a screw-up in the first few minutes of existence, but the nurses were telling me that everything was okay.

Fourteen hours earlier, at 4 a.m., Sophie's water had broken. It wasn't a gush like it would be for our second-born. It was a slow, controlled flow. She woke me up, told me we needed to go to the hospital, and asked me to consult the book *The Birth Partner*. She had bought it for me when we learned she was pregnant, and she'd trusted me to read it. I'd been meaning to each night, but I was always occupied with work or too tired. Finally, as the date approached, I took it to the office, planning to read a chapter each day at lunch. I'd left it at work and had to call Michel, our security guard at West Block, and ask him to please find it and send it home in a cab. I sped-read while Sophie dressed. She could have yelled at me and would have been justified about it, but she just shook her head sadly.

Six months earlier, Sophie had informed me she was going to get a doula, which as far as I could tell, was a fancy term for a midwife. It wasn't anything personal, she told me, it wasn't a lack of confidence, she just wanted someone with her, a woman, who knew what she was doing. I went along, naturally, and went to all the pre-natal classes. The first time the doula came to our home to meet with us, I felt relieved despite feeling somehow inadequate. The doula was jolly and physically imposing, like Mrs. Claus or a Babylonian fertility goddess with clothes, and in all her gestures and mannerisms she conveyed experience and reassurance. She and Sophie began to talk about the importance to a good birth of Kegels, the exercise where you tighten the muscles of your pelvic floor. At some point in the conversation the doula turned to me with a knowing look and told me I should try Kegels too. "They're very good for your prostate, and they help you *last* longer." She smiled. "And that of course is good" – and here she turned back to my wife – "for everyone." Of course it was.

I have to confess that when my wife went into labour and her Astarte doula happened to be out of town and her young doula back-up came along – the back-up who understood and could talk all the theory but who had never actually been alone at a birth – I was both nervous and relieved. And I am happy to report that I acquitted myself honourably on the delivery field of blood and sweat and tears. Apparently I did a good job with the back massaging, and hand and leg holding, and staying calm at the right times, and telling stories, and stroking Sophie's hair, and fetching towels and pillows.

Finally it was over. It was midnight, and Sophie and the baby were asleep. I wandered down to the hospital cafeteria to get a coffee and doughnut. A few years later, after the birth of our third child, I would do the same thing, except this time RIM would be a house-hold name. That time I wouldn't be sure if I was in the part of the hospital where I was allowed to use wireless devices, but I figured I wasn't going to cause all the dialysis machines to shut down, so I would surreptitiously BlackBerry the office while pretending to sip my coffee: "Baby born at 9 p.m. Boy. Named Benjamin. Eight pounds eight ounces. Mother and son doing well." A whole birth recorded and reported in under twenty words. Nearly instantaneous delivery of the message. Less than five minutes later Allan would reply: "Congratulations to you and Sophie. Now put down the BlackBerry and get back to your family." I would smile and obey.

Allan called me about something later that week. Our first baby was seventy-two hours old, and I was taking the week off but taking calls. Years later I don't remember what he called me about, only that he had to talk to me, and I was trying to give him advice while I had a screaming infant in my arms. I was pacing back and forth, because movement was the only thing that calmed our first-born down. Allan was laughing, and I could tell he didn't mind. After I put down the phone, Sophie asked me who had called, and when I told her it was Allan, she was embarrassed for me, but I told her not to worry. She cared enough about me that she fretted, but didn't care enough about what I did to be overly impressed. It was just like it was back at university. Back then I was writing her a new poem almost every week. She took each small offering the way a bored queen might accept a new island in her empire from her fondest privateer explorer. By the time of Allan's call, poems had given way to accounts of my day, and Sophie received each briefing with the same patience. But it was different for me.

Politics is the ideal drug for men because it is a cocktail of a simple desire for power and a complex quest to save the world. Every decision, every meeting, every utterance is pregnant with meaning, with consequence while you do the ancient, intricate, delicate democratic dance of leading and being led at the same time. Men remain boys for the whole of their lives because they always want to belong, to be part of a tribe, with its secret rituals and initiation rites and its stories of courage and triumph that are passed down from one generation to the next. Men always want to go down from wherever they are – mountain caves, mansions, skyscrapers – to spill blood on the battlefield, that of their enemies and their own.

Women are much wiser. They tolerate their men's passions for real or mediated violence with a knowing shrug, and then get on with the important things, like taking care of their children.

I would come home from work, and before I finished kissing Sophie and the children I would already be spilling stories of the heroic minutiae of my day: what so-and-so said, what so-and-so did, the jokes, the surprises, the adventures of travel, the setbacks, the cruel and inhumane scorched earth policies of the enemy, the wily stratagems we were putting into play to regain the power that we deserved. I was like an excited frat boy dressed in dark, grown-up suits and good shoes. At night, when we had put the children to sleep, and I had made Sophie tea, and as we lay in bed with the world compressed into a little ball, and as I stroked her arm, I would whisper to her the state secrets of the day and needlessly swear her to secrecy, needlessly because she loved me and would never betray my confidence – and because she wasn't really interested.

When I was a boy in elementary school, I couldn't wait to get to high school, because then I'd be big and grown up and could shave and drive a car. When I was in high school, I wanted to get to university so I could choose my own courses and have more time to write poetry and not have to obey so many stupid rules. After I reached university and left poetry behind, I wanted to graduate and get a job, start earning money, buy a car, and buy a nice house. When I met Sophie I wanted to get married. When I got married and bought a house, I wanted to start having kids and pay off the mortgage and do my job well.

I'm not sure if everyone lives their life this way, but I think most of us are more or less happy, more or less successful, more or less at peace with ourselves, our lives, and our God. And then one day we wake up and wonder where the time has gone. Before I knew it, fifteen years had gone by and I had three children, a beautiful wife, a house I wanted to grow old and die in, and the second best job in the country. For the first time in my life I wanted time to stand still.

As I got older, my relationship with time changed in other ways. When I was younger I would lose hundreds of hours a year to meetings, perhaps thousands of hours. Meetings where people would talk to hear themselves talk, where smart, articulate people would say the same things over and over again, as if they confused repetition with argumentation and logic, and where nothing was decided, and worse still, nothing was learned. I also spent more time than I can remember sitting through speeches – not Allan's – that were devoid of surprise, that gave you no reason to attend, because you could predict almost every word that would be said based on who was speaking and what was going on in the news, whether it was singing their own praises or damning an opponent's program or character or motives, and where, because of this lack of suspense, the words lost their power to thrill.

I eventually stopped attending these speeches and meetings, and when I found myself in the middle of a session where my presence was unnecessary and where I could neither bring nor derive any benefit, I'd stand up in the middle of the conversation, wish everyone luck, offer up my time at some later point, and politely exit. I stopped going out to cocktail parties that I didn't want to go to, that I'd attended before out of a sense of politeness or duty. I stopped reading books because I felt I had to. The fact that certain books represented huge gaps in my reading and education, like *War and Peace*, or mocked me in their absence, like James Joyce's *Ulysses*, no longer bothered me. If I were reading a book that felt like duty rather than pleasure, like medicine rather than mead, I would stop, even if I were only a few pages in. And I began to forgive myself in advance for the fact I would probably never get around to reading all the books I had heard about and wanted to read, like *The Life and Opinions of Tristram Shandy, Gentleman.* I stopped worrying about many things that used to keep me up at night, as each worry slipped away in the fact of it not coming true. I stopped being dissatisfied with my imperfections and learned to appreciate and tolerate them, if not to love them. To my delight, I learned I could do many things faster, and better, whether it was thinking or reading or writing.

Like many men in their late thirties, I took up jogging, which may seem paradoxical, because it involved moving faster when what I really wanted was to slow down. But I took up jogging precisely because, like so many others, I wanted to slow down time, or at least outrace it for a few years. At first I was pretty bad, and I only went out at night, so that I wouldn't be recognized gasping my way along Ottawa's clean streets or along the Rideau Canal, walking in between short bouts of running. But over the course of one long summer, I grew into a proficient jogger. It became one of my most anticipated activities of the day and of my middle age.

After I became good at it, I would start off early in the morning, leaving from our A-frame house in the southern part of the Glebe. I'd make my way east along the two blocks to the Canal and then turn left and run north along Colonel By. I would pass the beautiful brick and stone homes that stolidly overlooked the Canal, up to the National War Memorial where just across Rideau Street the Canal's locks down below separated the light Château Laurier from the dark East Block.

For my thirty-eighth birthday, in 2003, Sophie got me one of the early iPods, and I played some of my favourite music as I ran: the Police, The Clash, Bob Marley. The music of my youth. The music that has the biggest impact on you is what you listen to in your teenage years. That's when everything is happening to you for the first time and you have so much time to waste that one of the most important questions you can ask one another is, "So what kind of music do you like?" As I hit my forties, my iPod would come to include the non-threatening rhymes of Coldplay, which Sophie disparagingly referred to as middle-aged men's music.

I would see the usual few other cyclists and joggers making their way in the morning, and we would exchange polite Ottawa waves or nods. And then I would return the same way to shower, eat, and dress for work. Every year, during the few short weeks from January to late February when the Canal froze over and was open to skaters, I would trade my running shoes for my old skates, and skate to work. After a couple of years I surprised myself by becoming a passable skater.

For the first few minutes of running, my mind would empty and I would think of nothing except putting one foot in front of the other, adjusting to the impact of my joints on concrete, feeling my breathing increase in strength and rhythm. Once I was under way, my mind would refill, pleasantly, as with warm water for a bath, and the problems of the day before, or the upcoming ones of the current day would rearrange themselves from dark shadows into bright clear shapes that I could manage. Sometimes as I jogged along the Canal, my mind would revert to my youth.

In the early years, when I was learning my profession, every situation, every challenge, every decision was new. There was no mental filing cabinet of experience to draw on — every new situation had to be analyzed and cross-referenced with the instincts that I had and that I was carefully learning to develop. My goal in the first five years of my career was to learn as much as I could without making a fatal mistake. To make up for my lack of experience, I had to work harder, working twelve to fifteen hour days, taking the extra time to think through scenarios and alternatives. If we took such and such a position, how would the public react? And every second event was a crisis — all of us were young, and everything was new, and like young soldiers serving on their first tour of duty in the jungle, every makeshift bomb, every ambush, every noise was a major event.

After a while, if you survive that critical apprenticeship, you start to be able to put things in perspective, to understand that not every firefight is a major battle. And you recognize the best hope you have of staying alive when the air around you is filled with the randomness of death is to stay calm and rational. There is a place for emotion – without it you would never step out of the safety and warmth of your tent into the darkness – but if you let emotions overwhelm you, then you will make mistakes. You will misread the signs or miss them altogether, or you will not be patient – you will rush toward your objective and step on that metaphorical mine.

I remember being at one of my first press conferences. Allan was announcing funding for a new senior's centre in our Defence Minister's riding in Ottawa West – Nepean, and Michael was there. He asked me if I knew what he was going to write. I thought that would be presumptuous and said no. He looked at me with something like professional pity and told me I should get to the point where I knew exactly how every story would turn out, based on our message, the context, and the reporter. I thought that was farfetched, but politely, humbly, inoffensively thanked him for his insight.

Early in my career I often found my ability to speak well could be influenced by stress and lack of sleep. I'd misspeak, use the wrong word, leave out an article or a conjunction, trip over my words or use fillers, like, "you know," "I guess," "sort of," like a reasonably intelligent but inarticulate university student. As I got older, I learned to speak more slowly, to give my mouth time to catch up to my brain. Occasionally, when I was pressed for time, or was sensitive to Allan's time, I'd try to speak quickly and trip over my words. At other times I would express my thoughts in more of a rushing stream of consciousness than anything approaching numbered or bulleted simplicity. I took an executive speaking course where the instructor told us that people who had high status and who wanted to be seen as important, and therefore taken seriously, never spoke quickly. They spoke slowly, because what they had to say was worth hearing, and they knew that their audience knew this and would listen to them.

Allan once told me over a few beers that I needed to be more verbally concise, and I took the constructive criticism seriously. I also learned that while content and results were obviously important, how my advice was delivered in times of crisis or even tension was as important to Allan as my actual counsel, maybe more important. Although we wore suits and shaved and washed, and although our only weapons were the words we cleaned and polished and carried and aimed and fired, we were at war, and Allan had no time for drama.

Plans, recommendations, assessments, facts, cautions, summaries, all had to be delivered in the calm tones of a surgeon explaining tomorrow's brain surgery to his patient, or asking for a scalpel the next day in the operating room. Empathetic, yes, but also authoritative and calm, cold and cleansing as a stream during the winter run-off. Sometimes I thought I got my job with Allan, and held on to it for years, not because I had any particular gift with words or strategy but because of the way I was able to appear. I could appear (though certainly not necessarily be or feel) so comfortingly calm under pressure that could very quickly shut down your ability to think. I had earned, and continued to deserve my job, not through any innate talent or acquired proficiency in my field, but by virtue of an inability to display panic. It was a skill I had learned as I traded in my books and my poetic ambitions for what passed for real life in politics.

In the late eighties and early nineties, as Glasnost and Perestroika changed our conception of history, and as the Berlin Wall came down, I often found myself wondering how a man like Gorbachev survived for thirty years in a system that he would one day, once he achieved power, tear apart like a blinded Samson bringing the temple down on his head.

Did he quietly go into work each day, make small and big decisions, and invest his passion in everything he didn't believe in? As he rose steadily through Party ranks, did his chauffeur and his dacha bring comfort or distraction from all the greyness around him? Did he believe in the system for most of the beginning of his career, only to have an epiphany one day that it was rotten, without a future, and had to change? Or did his doubt start slowly, like a small insurrection in a border province, perhaps while he drove by a group of his comrades waiting in line for hours for toilet paper, or one day over coffee as he read the made-up news in *Pravda*, and grow bit by bit each day without him really noticing until he had no choice but to act? How does a man like this ever win the leadership of his Party?

Allan was no Gorbachev – he wasn't bringing down a system, he didn't doubt our Party's ideology, and we didn't have as many obvious gulags – but in our early years we navigated our way through the Party the way I imagined Gorbachev might have survived in the USSR. In Allan's first years as an MP, we kept our profile just high enough to make progress, but not so high as to attract anyone's undue attention. We were careful to help everyone and offend no one. We disagreed when we had to, but we found a way to never say no outright, and we made it hard for anyone, either across the floor or within the Party, to really dislike Allan. We stayed clear of partisanship, ideology, personal attacks. We didn't attempt any grand policies or manoeuvres or take big risks. We kept our heads down and steered clear of mistakes. By the end of his second term, in 1994, Allan had developed a reputation for sure-footed political instincts, competence, and an ability to connect with people.

ALLAN

Sixteen years after I was first elected, and the day after I won the leadership race, Eli came into my office and dropped a CD on my desk. We had both been in the office since 7 a.m., and he was interrupting my careful reading of the leadership transition briefing documents. I'd only had about two hours sleep, but already the previous night's victory was a distant memory. I remembered a few things, like Katherine smiling and standing beside me and holding my hand as the final ballots were tallied in the convention centre, and Eli on the other side, arms pumping the air like a prizefighter's ecstatic cornerman, and my father standing next to Eli. My father was clapping and fighting back the tears I had only ever seen in his eyes once before, when his mother died before her time. I was smiling and waving and looking good for the cameras, but all I could help thinking was that I somehow didn't deserve it, that I was too young. And although any normal human being would have been enjoying himself, relishing the moment, my Presbyterian genes were in complete control, and my thoughts were already focused on the next race.

Eli sat down across from me. "Please watch this at home."

He looked uncharacteristically nervous, so I glanced at the CD and returned to my reading. "What is it?"

"It's the first cut of our first-ever *assertive* ads." He was being clever with words and I wondered, for the first time ever, if I'd misplaced my trust in him.

I put down the papers. "Eli, years ago you and I decided we'd never run attack ads. This is anthrax. Why are you giving it to me?" I was speaking to him like my father used to talk to me when I was

119

a boy and was being disobedient, and he was trying to sound caring and reasonable.

"I remember our position when we were starting off. Just hear me out. For the sake of argument."

I signaled okay with a dip of my chin.

"You agree that attack ads will be run against us?"

"Yes."

"Do you remember the Willie Horton ad?"

I nodded, but grudgingly.

"Do you remember the swiftboating of John Kerry?"

I nodded again.

"Do you agree that attack ads work?"

I didn't like being led to conclusions like a donkey to water. "I'll admit they've worked in the past. However, I'd argue that in both those cases, the Democrats made the fatal error of not responding quickly enough and hard enough. They let the negative framing of their policies and character stand."

"You're right, but no matter how quickly or effectively you respond, you are *responding*. You're going second. You're on the defensive. You're playing black in a chess game. You're working hard to tell people that you are not a crook. And once you are called a crook out loud, it never leaves the public's mind, no matter how hard, and sometimes because of how hard, you work to refute it." Eli's initial nervousness was gone. He was speaking passionately but logically, not trying too hard to sell. He was confident in his recommendation.

"Eli, what are you suggesting?" My voice was soft.

"Do you agree that the other side will run attack ads, that they will paint you as too young, too ambitious, a rich Daddy's boy out of touch with ordinary Canadians?"

I felt nauseous, and I think it showed on my face. "I agree."

"Neither you nor I ever wanted to do attack ads. We don't want to do them today. It's not who we are. But if we don't tell our story first we're never going to have a chance."

"Why can't we tell our story without going on the attack?"

"We have to put the Government on the defensive and give ourselves room to tell Canadians who we are. Just two ads, portraying the Government as out of touch, aloof, past their prime, tired, with no vision and no ambition except to get re-elected. Then we will have bought ourselves enough time and space to tell our story."

I looked at him for a while. He stared back, didn't break his gaze. "You have obviously thought about this. Everyone on the leadership team supports?"

"Yes."

I returned to my reading. "Let me think about it." I wasn't looking forward to discussing this idea of Eli's with Katherine. I knew Katherine would not approve. She believed good leaders won on what they stood for, not on what they stood against. She was convinced attack ads were the single biggest cause of voter cynicism, and she wouldn't want me to be associated with them. I also knew that she would trust me if I decided to act on Eli's recommendation.

Eli stood up to go. "Okay, but I'd like to start running the ads no later than next week. And we're going to need to raise a lot of money to pay for them. Quickly."

I said nothing. Just waited for him to leave.

MICHAEL

Four weeks into his tenure as Leader of the Party, Allan set out to restore the Party's depleted finances in that great ritual of modern democracy, the fundraiser. Toronto Convention Centre, tables of ten, a thousand dollars a plate. At first the dinner was to be closed to the media, so I hadn't planned on going, but in the final seventy-two hours the organizers had a change of heart. Those of us in the fourth estate were eager to glimpse Allan in action soon after becoming leader, but what had really caught our interest was the press release five days before the event. The former PM, Edward Laffrey, who hadn't given a speech in nearly six years, was to be the keynote speaker. [Edward Laffrey had served as PM for three terms before admirably concluding he would probably not win a fourth term, gracefully bowing out in favour of his anointed successor. Like so many political leaders succeeding a strong personality who had held a long mandate, Laffrey's successor Alex Chambers would go on to convincingly lose the next election. This unintentional self-immolation at the ballot box would conveniently pave the way for Allan's leadership victory in 2002.] We lowly scribes were seated together at two tables at the back, as usual, where we couldn't embarrass anyone, not even ourselves.

My wife, Meredith, a well-regarded and borderline workaholic in-house general counsel for one of the big phone companies, was also in attendance, but sitting with other executives at her company's table. Her table was two rows in front and three tables to my left. To my eternal embarrassment, ever since I had met her in Ottawa when I was still at the *Citizen* and she was an articling student,

122

Meredith had been a card-carrying member of Allan's Party. She had joined its youth wing when she was in grade ten. Halfway through the dinner I went over to speak to her, and even though her colleagues knew me, their conversation became a little less merry when I reached their table, as if they were worried I might overhear them saying something I would not be able to resist using in my story.

I had chosen my seat at the media table so I could see Meredith's profile when she was watching the speakers at the podium, and I felt a pang of something uncomfortable but familiar when I saw how much she smiled at Allan while he was speaking. It was like she was a reasonably self-contained teenager watching a beloved boy band perform. But I love my wife, despite my own failings, and she appears to love me, although she claims to have no time for the children I think I want to have.

It seemed like everybody in the Party was there, along with everyone in the business community. These last were either loyal supporters who had been so during the years of exile, neutrals supporting the democratic process and hedging their bets, or, those who wore their ambition on their well-fed faces. The latter were like small-time kings in satellite states who sensed a shift in political momentum in faraway Rome and wanted to get in on the winning side before the battle that would decide the next emperor.

I knew a lot of people in the crowd: Cabinet ministers, Party hangers-on, flacks, and many of the senior executives who kept Canadian finance and industry on the rails. Businesspeople are very different from political ones. Their rituals are more ambiguous, their lines of authority clearer, their distance from the front greater. Business requires a different kind of leadership. This is painfully proven by the number of very successful business leaders who make the existential leap off the stone cliff of commerce into the thin air of politics, only to find they never develop the instincts or can't adjust to the incredible inefficiencies in terms of making decisions when you can no longer dictate from the head of the boardroom table. Those who take the plunge often come across like kings coming down to play at being prime minister. They're always in a huff, always impatient at having to woo the great unwashed electorate, whereas before they could quietly and easily rule over their vast, often multinational empires.

These fundraising fandangos normally follow a predictable pattern – a long drawn-out meal followed by rambling, unsubtle partisan speeches – but the former PM needed to be on his way to France, no doubt to lobby for some client in the great long afterlife of politics, so the speeches came first. Jean Prud'homme, Opposition Finance Critic, introduced Allan with all the appropriate humour, but early on it was very clear this was a rally to get the troops ready for the war and the election that was three years away. Jean was part field general, part hockey announcer as he called out the names of the party heavyweights and asked them to stand to raucous applause. By the time he called on Allan to come to the front of the room, the crowd was ready to leap over the trenches, and the room burst into loud clapping and the first of many standing ovations when Jean introduced Allan as our "next Prime Minister."

The head table – with Jean, Allan, Allan's father, the former PM Laffrey, and their wives – had been situated strategically, not at the front of the room, but in the centre, so that Allan had to pass several tables as he slowly made his way to the podium. As he walked, you would have thought he was already the Prime Minister from the way he smiled and the way everyone in his path stood up to greet him, shake his hand, and say their names in the most memorable way they could manage.

When Allan reached the podium, he smiled, gripped it firmly, and looked out at the heaving crowd. He raised his hand in acknowledgement of the welcome, the hope, the desire to regain the seat of power, and nodded, shyly and in gratitude. I could see his lips moving on the wide screens at the two front corners of the room – *Thank you, thank you* – and thought of a blond, more restrained, more powerful Elvis Presley.

"Thank you very much for that warm welcome," he managed to say when the applause had died down. "Tonight is a very special night for all of us. It's the night when we begin our journey back to being in government, the night when we return to being able to serve all Canadians, not just special interest groups, or regions, or narrow causes that don't appeal to our best selves. I want to thank you for being here, and thank you for your generous support. I also want to promise that we will not let you down, that we will restore Canada to its rightful position as a leader in the world, not just economically, but socially, culturally, environmentally, and morally.

"Our first priority when we form government will be to bring back to Canada the fiscal discipline that was a hallmark of the government led by Prime Minister Laffrey –" he paused here for loud appreciative applause," – and we will use our newfound economic strength to take the right positions on all the issues that the current government is refusing to lead on. We will adopt what makes the most sense from the US but we will not follow them blindly. We will honour our environmental commitments and we will build our international trade relationships. We will increase support to the arts, which have caused the writing and art and films and music of Canadians to be read and seen and heard around the world. We will restore the pride and standing of our fine military, which we depend on to defend our country and our freedom. And we will champion the traditional Canadian values that we all share. We will take back our Canada.

"But before we do, I want to introduce you to the passionate leader and very special Canadian who has made it possible for us to be here today. Without him, our Canada would be a very different place. It's my very great pleasure to introduce a man who needs no introduction, a man who has given his life to public service, who has never ceased to remind us that Canada is the best country in the world, that even when we have challenges and problems, we are blessed to have the challenges and problems we have, who has never stopped fighting for the ordinary Canadian, who has never shied away from doing the right thing: ladies and gentlemen, Prime Minister Laffrey."

Eli was sitting just one table over from the head table, and from where I was sitting I could see the back of his head with just a bit of his right cheek and the tip of his nose. I could have sworn he nodded slightly when Allan had finished speaking. Before we had sat down for dinner, when Meredith was spending quality time with her CEO, everyone else was talking away madly in the hall-way reception outside the ballroom, and quiet waiters in black were flitting around offering hors d'oeuvres and glasses of wine, I had walked over to Eli. He was standing a respectable distance of about fifteen feet from Allan. Allan appeared relaxed, as usual, and seemed to be telling funny stories to the CEOs of two of our major banks. Eli was engaged in what looked like serious conversation with a couple of his Party's political staffers.

The two staffers looked like they were in first-year university, at the same time too young for their jobs, with their unlined skin and nervous energy, and too old for their ages, with their cheap black pinstriped suits and cell phones. If I squinted or ignored their suits and hungry looks, they reminded me of Allan, Eli, and my-self back at McGill before everything went wrong between us. Eli was speaking with them, but he was also watching Allan carefully, like a parent chaperoning his adolescent son at a dance or a horse trainer nervously eyeing his animal in between races. He didn't see me come up beside him. I startled him when I said, "Hello," but he recovered quickly.

"Hi Michael. Michael, this is Don and this is John. Don, John, this is an old friend." We all shook hands. I almost made a joke about "Don Juan" but restrained myself. "Be careful what you say around him, though," Eli said to Don Juan. "He's on the dark side. He's a journalist." We all laughed, but Don and John looked at me reproachfully. An uncharacteristically daring part of me wanted to ask Eli how Sophie was, but by this time I'd forgotten how to have a personal conversation with him, so I asked him instead if he thought Allan would unseat the PM in the next election. As questions go, it was a dumb one, because there was only one politically correct answer that Eli could give me. Which he did without any effort. "Of course. Canadians are looking for a change." I didn't bother writing it down, and I never found out if I would have asked Eli about Sophie because they started ushering us in to dinner.

If Allan's stroll to the front of the room was an enthusiastic coronation, by the way the crowd jumped to its feet, began applauding as one, and chanted "Laf-frey, Laff-rey," drawing out the final syllable with a roar as Laffrey made his way to the podium, the former PM's presence was like the return of a political demi-god. Laffrey would have been over seventy then, but you would have thought he was a man in his prime, in his well-fitting suit, by the way he moved through the crowd, a running back in slow motion, shaking hands, clapping and being clapped on the back, waving to people at various tables, his hair still thick, his handshake still firm, his toothy smile still shooting off electricity halfway across the room. The roar only got louder when he reached the stage and chose to stand a little to the side of the podium, with a wireless lapel microphone, and several times tried to quiet the crowd. It was the political version of a rock concert, and I half expected some of the serious men in the front row to swoon, or Laffrey to jump into the crowd and bodysurf on a wave of outstretched hands. Finally, after what must have been four minutes of cheering, the crowd finally was seated and silent.

Like every skilled speaker, Laffrey didn't just dive right in, but started slowly, dipping his toe in the emotion of the crowd, letting them come to him as much as he came to them. He started with his trademark growl, the enunciation and cadences of the anti-orator who was so skilled at communicating with every audience that he could break all the rules, slurring words, speaking in a dull drone that evoked the brilliance and attraction of Leonard Cohen's monotone baritone, avoiding the studied hand gestures that men who would lead other men have copied since Pericles and Cicero. I'd seen him speak and reported on it countless times when he'd ruled Canada as a democratically elected despot, and I'd never become bored by how he could seize the attention of a crowd, almost like the wrestler he had been in college, with his fists and thick arms, or at other times like a ballet dancer holding his partner in a delicate grip of iron and taking her from point A to point B in the opposite of a straight line.

"Good evening, Ladies and Gentlemen. As you know, I haven't given a speech in six years, so I apologize if I'm rusty, but when Allan called and asked me if I would speak here this evening, how could I refuse? Allan's father Alex and I served together in five governments. He was one of my most important ministers in our three consecutive mandates. There is no better friend I could have had in my many years of politics. It was Alex who encouraged me to run for the leadership when everybody who knows about such things said I was too old-fashioned, too out of touch with the modern world that was supposedly our Canada. But Alex came to see me, and he convinced me to run." And then Laffrey looked over at Allan's father, seated at the head table, and said quietly, so that the impression was that only Alex Keyes could hear it, "Thank you."

"Over the years, we have fought our battles together and won our victories together, but tonight, Alex and I are the old soldiers on the sidelines. We have done our fighting for Canada. Today is a new day, and today Alex's fine son Allan is your leader. I can say, without equivocation, that you have made a great choice. You have chosen a true leader, and after forty years in the rough and tumble of politics, I have found that there is no challenge that true leadership cannot overcome, and there is no way to avoid failure without leadership. Allan is a man of integrity, and we have all seen this integrity in the realm of politics from day one, when Allan refused my offer to run in his father's riding, a safe riding if there ever was one, and chose instead to run in Rosemont – La Petite-Patrie, where he was unknown."

When I'd heard Allan would be running in that riding and not in his father's safe one, I had thought it was a beyond reckless opening gambit in what would turn out to be a very short political career. It was like moving your queen out too early in chess. (But there is a reason that some people go into politics and some into journalism.) Allan had also seized the moment when he ran for the leadership. Everyone thought he was too young, but all the heavy hitters in Cabinet who should have been shoo-ins for the leadership decided to sit out the leadership contest because they felt the PM was unbeatable. Three years later Allan would reap the benefits of their miscalculations.

"Many thought he was being foolish, overly proud, reckless even, but what looked like recklessness to us old men has proven to be the strongest character. As a backbencher, Allan did not rest on his father's laurels, nor did he expect to be handed the proverbial silver spoon. He started before 7 a.m. and worked harder than all of us, not leaving the office each night until nine, ten, eleven o'clock, and never before his job was done." [This was true. Allan would go in early to the office, usually by 6.30 a.m. and would leave late. It appeared to voters that he was both dedicated and superhuman. But he had a comfortable couch in his office, and every day between 1 and 1.30 p.m. when he was in Ottawa he would take a nap. I learned this once from one of my key contacts in the PMO. Not Eli, obviously.]

"He made a difference in Ottawa on a national level, working on various important files, but he never lost sight of the ordinary Canadian in his riding, was never too busy to meet with a constituent, or answer a letter, or take a phone call in the middle of the night. He never lost sight of the fact that he had been given an opportunity in life that not all Canadians have. He never took this for granted, and he never ceased to work hard to level the playing field for all Canadians, so that all Canadians might have the opportunities he was given."

It went on this vein for another fifteen minutes, and when Laffrey was finished, the standing ovation began. It carried on as Laffrey left the stage, and made his way back to the table, where he sat down and everyone congratulated him on the best political speech of the year. Allan raised $1.1 million that night. I've written down the speech as I best remember it. I've chosen not to consult any tapes or check against delivery texts, because I wanted to relive the moment as I recall it, not necessarily how it was exactly, and I have never included in any of my reporting or columns what I am about to share here, because I'm not sure if my perceptions reveal more about the event or more about me.

Although I get paid to listen to these things, at a certain point in the speech what Laffrey was saying stopped having a specific meaning for me: Laffrey could have been speaking Greek or Latin or Norse or any other ancient language. I stopped hearing the words. The convention ballroom melted away, and all I saw were coarse wooden beams or a tent on some windswept beach, the longboats or triremes in the water and ready to sail at dawn. Instead of clean-shaven men in suits, I saw men with beards dressed in armour, drinking to steel their courage, and above all, men ready to go to war and lay down their lives for their leader and their ideals, whatever they might be.

ELI

"How many of you have ever heard of Joseph Campbell?" asked the man standing at the front of the conference room in the North Hatley Inn in Quebec's Eastern Townships. Allan and I raised our hands halfway. So did one or two others. I could see the July sun reflecting off Lake Massawippi through the window behind our guest speaker. "Not Ki-im," the vowel drawn out forever in the speaker's Southern US accent, a finger wagging naughtily. "Joseph. Joseph Campbell wrote *The Hero with a Thousand Faces*. He studied myths from all periods of our history, and from all cultures, and over the course of many years he discovered something very interesting. We tend to think, perhaps even *like* to think that our own myths and stories are unique, totally unlike any other myths and stories in any other time or place. Do you know what Campbell found?"

Transported back to university or high school, we obediently shook our heads and murmured, "No."

The man standing at the front of the room smiled. His name was Jesse Halliwell. A political and communications strategist who had grown up writing articles and books in the safe harbour of the University of Alabama, he had been a complete unknown until he left the ivory tower to help lead another complete unknown to the presidency of the United States. Because our Party and his were political cousins, he'd graciously agreed to waive his usual $50,000-a-day fee to come to the Eastern Townships to address our three-day strategic planning retreat where we were drawing up our blueprint for our return to power.

"He found that though we think there are thousands of unique

131

myths on our planet, we actually only have one "monomyth" that is told in different ways at different times. He calls this the Hero's Journey. This is the story that George Lucas popularized, got down to a science, if you will, and in so doing forever changed the face of American cinema – for better or worse, depending on your point of view. And do you know who Lucas had working with him as a special adviser on *Star Wars*? That's right, Joseph Campbell.

"Who remembers the beginning of *Star Wars*?" More hands are raised this time. Instead of grown, serious men thinking about and preparing for serious things, we are early adolescents playing with our light sabers and dreaming of saving the universe. Back in the seventies we all wanted to be Luke Skywalker. I found myself wondering why every boy today dreams of being Darth Vader or Darth Sidious.

"Excellent." Big smile. "If you recall, Luke is on the planet Tatooine with his uncle and aunt. He is a humble farmer, doing ordinary work. Lucas is setting the scene, sketching the context us for us. He is saying to us, 'You are here, in this particular time and place.'

"The next phase is when Luke encounters the holographic SOS from Princess Leia. This is the *Call to Adventure*, an early but a critical juncture. If Luke doesn't take up the call to adventure, there is no story. The story ends.

"Next, Luke must rally a team of people around him who also believe in his quest. His team begins with a few irascible androids, but then grows to encompass Obi-Wan Kenobi and Han Solo: brains and brawn at first, but really wisdom and street smarts, or idealism and realism. Obi-Wan is driven by the purest of motives; Han Solo, at least at first, is motivated by money. You need both if you want to succeed in politics."

Laughter.

"What comes next of course is the confrontation, the battle, or series of conflicts, with the enemy. And, as we all know, to be a great hero, you need a great enemy. Can anybody say Darth Vader?

132

And finally, in all good quests, that is, in all quests that end well, the hero and his team need to accomplish their mission: to defeat evil and discover or recover what they've been looking for. In the case of *Star Wars*, two of mankind's greatest and oldest objectives: to find and/or free a woman and to win freedom.

"Now, you're probably all wondering, all well and good, Jesse, but what in the hell is Jesse Halliwell doing on a nice sunny day talking about *Star Wars*? What do *Star Wars* and Joseph Campbell and myth have to do with the down and dirty business of winning elections? In fact, a lot. All of you are already well on your way on your quest, which is to return to power as the Government of Canada. You have a hero," he nodded at Allan, "you have a call to adventure, and you have the beginnings of a team. Thanks to your fundraising efforts, you have a substantial war chest. Now, all you have to do is take your call to action and articulate it in simple terms that tens of millions of people can understand, feel an emotional connection to, and rally behind. You have a lot of challenges in front of you."

It appeared that a lot had changed since I went to university in the early eighties. Stories then were something that you read in books or told each other or watched at the movies. By the beginning of the twenty-first century they were strategies used by corporations and political parties to make money and win elections. Although I had to pay attention to what Canada's political and business journalists were writing by the day and, increasingly, by the hour, with each passing year I found myself turning more and more to the arts pages when I first picked up my morning newspapers. I still had a fondness for good old-fashioned stories.

"Let me just state the most obvious: there's the sitting government, and the Prime Minister that you have to defeat, and the challenges inherent in the position of Opposition in a parliamentary system, where you have no access to the thousands of civil servants that the government has at its command – it really is a democratic dictatorship. But your real enemy, the one you have to come to terms with, the one you have to understand as well as you understand your own psyche, and then slay, is inertia. Indifference."

We had scheduled the session with Jesse Halliwell for 9.30 a.m., but had told Allan it started at 9 so maybe he would be on time. And he was. It was a trick that all of us who worked with Allan came upon sooner or later. Allan had never had a lot of use for being on time at university, which was fairly standard, but while the rest of us had grown up and started wearing watches and caring about getting to places on time, Allan regressed, almost to a state of childhood where activities simply blended into each other with no real start or end or transition. Meetings never started or ended on time and, very quickly, we had all learned to look out for him. At first glance it was a flaw, but when you saw him on the campaign trail or meeting with a constituent, you realized it was also one of his greatest gifts.

When you're interviewing someone for a job, one of the basic questions is to ask them to describe their greatest strength and weakness. It has become such an expected part of a job interview that most people prepare for it. The most unintentionally funny answer, the one people think you want to hear, is that they're a workaholic or a perfectionist who cares too much about work for their own good. But I've always believed that generally people don't have strengths or weaknesses. They have qualities that are both strengths and weaknesses. Some people's greatest strength is that they are thoughtful. They think everything through before making a decision, and as a result they almost always make the right decision. But their need to take the time to think everything through is also their greatest weakness because sometimes they don't act fast enough and so miss opportunities. So it was with Allan and time. Allan never made anyone who was with him feel like he was pressed for time. He made everyone feel special, as if he had all the time in the world for them, and I suppose in a sense he did.

"Indifference. Every day, each of us is bombarded with over ten thousand messages: verbal, oral, visual, even smell and touch. These are messages from our wives, girlfriends, husbands, friends, teachers, church, TV, radio, iPods, billboards, the Internet, newspapers, advertising in the urinals, books. Never before has there been so much information and so little time to absorb it. Everyone is multitasking, emailing when they're talking on the phone, looking at their BlackBerries instead of paying attention to the person speaking in a meeting, listening to music when they're jogging, watching TV when they're doing their homework or interacting with their families. Distraction is the dominant theme of our society.

"Most of the time, people are thinking about what to eat for dinner, whether they're going to have sex that night, how they're going to redecorate their kitchen, what car they're going to buy, what song they're going to download, what they're going to buy or put on eBay, who won the hockey game last night, who's going to win tomorrow, how their kids are doing in school, how long the line-up at Tim Hortons is going to be today, how the market is treating their mutual funds, whether they can get tickets to the premiere of whatever. And these are the people who vote, the professional and academic and business class who traditionally are the foundation of democracies. Thanks to all the technology that was supposed to make our lives easier, coupled with our almost pathological expectations and our new religion of materialism, these people have almost no time to think about society and politics and making the world a better place beyond the limits of their nuclear families. The people who almost never vote are thinking about how they are going to pay their rent, buy food, and clothe their kids."

It was at this point that our foreign affairs critic Jerome Whitehouse chose to ask a question. "This is all great, Jesse, impressive really, but what does it mean for us in Canada?" Jerome was one of those people who liked to hear themselves talk and who never wanted for an opinion, regardless of the subject. The conviction with which he promoted his views was usually in inverse order to his level of knowledge. He talked the way he walked, with a swagger: shoulders thrown back, pelvis and chest thrust out, arms and legs akimbo. Yeats must have envisioned him when he wrote "The best lack all conviction, while the worst are full of passionate intensity."

Liking the sound of your own voice and having unlimited opinions on too many issues can be a prerequisite for success in politics, but the way Jerome did it, even when we were at a retreat, with no reporters or voters to score points with, was unique in our caucus. It was as if he had read one of those management self-help books that advised people who wanted to get ahead to always speak up loudly in meetings. Of course I had a bias. Despite his flaws, Jerome had come a close second to Allan in the leadership race, and he had never quite fallen into line behind him. But he had a following, and one of the most critical political lessons Allan had taught me was to have as many friends and as few enemies as possible. Without bothering to look at him, a few of his colleagues shook their heads at the way he had interrupted our guest speaker. Not a small number of others, however, were nodding their heads at Jerome's latest display of alpha maleness.

From Halliwell's reaction, you could tell he was used to being in the same room as people who liked to hear themselves talk. But he was human. The anger at being so boldly questioned and challenged in mid-stride appeared and then vanished across his eyes like a bird diving for a fish, so quickly that you questioned yourself whether you had actually seen it. He smiled, and said, "What does it have to do with Canada?" Long pause. "Only everything." He resumed speaking, and regained control of the room.

"Almost nobody *in Canada* – well-off or not – thinks about fiscal imbalance, or structural deficits, or fiscal policy, or punitive trade practices, or the growing productivity gap, or the brain drain, or first past the post versus proportional representation, the true cost of infrastructure, the rates of illiteracy and substance abuse in some native communities. Do you know how much time the average Canadian spends thinking about politics in the course of a week? Let's see a show of hands. Who says an hour? Okay. Who says more than an hour? Okay, thank you. Now, who are the really cynical in the room – who says less than an hour?"

Nobody raised their hand. Big smile. Flash of perfectly white teeth. "Everybody listen carefully: the answer is humbling." He held up seven fingers. "Seven minutes. Two minutes on municipal politics, two minutes on provincial politics, two minutes on federal politics. And, because Canadians do think about the world outside their borders, one minute on international politics. Harsh, isn't it? This is what you are up against. You have two minutes a week to win over the hearts and minds of Canadians."

Halfway though Halliwell's talk, I looked over at Allan. He'd cocked his head to one side, and his eyes were focused on the front of the room, where Halliwell was standing. Allan was nodding and smiling in the right places. To anybody else, it would have looked like he was fully attentive, but I could tell he was thinking of other things. He was holding his chin with his right hand, between his thumb and index finger, and stroking his skin with his finger, which, ever since I first met him at McGill, was a sure sign that his mind was wandering. I'd never told him this because with most people it was a sign of concentration, so it was harmless, and because I had to keep some things in reserve. Allan was probably thinking about tomorrow and the day after that and the next day. He always knew what he needed to know and do, and whom he needed around him to make it happen. The only times I saw him stop thinking about his next move was when he drove or water-skied or played rugby, which he still did once a week, on one of the Ottawa Irish Rugby Club's senior teams. Like a shark, he was only at peace when he was moving.

Halliwell was impressing most of the people in the room, a handful of whom were gifted politicians, the rest hardworking or well-connected or just lucky, winning a seat or a spot in Cabinet when the electoral tide or the brutal demographic mathematics of Cabinet making swept them along and lifted them up, but I could tell Allan wasn't impressed. He had already heard, if not already thought about, most of what Halliwell was offering. But unlike Whitehouse, Allan would never ask a question to make himself sound smarter than the speaker or anyone else in the room. He would let his caucus get what they could out of the speech, and at the end, he would smile and thank Halliwell for coming and sharing his wisdom and me for organizing the session. And then he would move on.

Halliwell was in full rhetorical stride at that point. There wasn't a note or PowerPoint slide in sight. Pacing back and forth. Head down. Not looking at the audience. Poor posture. Occasional slurring of vowels, often dropping the Gs. "People have no patience anymore. They want everything in their life to be like fast food. Publicly traded companies can no longer afford to take a long-term view, and decisions are made not in the best long-term interests of all stakeholders, but in the short-term interests of speculators who are out to make a quick buck, long-term value creation be damned. Politics in democratic societies is, by nature and design, short term – every four years you get a chance to turf out the bums – and most really good decisions will not bring dividends under the watch of the government that made them.

"You all know the stats because you live them every day. In fact, you help create them. The average sound bite in 1968 was 43 seconds. It's now down to nine. You have less time to communicate than ever before, paradoxically at a time when the challenges we face and the decisions we have to make are more complex than they have ever been. In this battle, and that's what it is, images are important because they communicate with a speed and power that words can't aspire to. This is no surprise. Depending on what continent your ancestors found themselves in when they climbed down from the trees or shambled out of the caves, you've been reading and writing for anywhere from four thousand to five hundred years. You've been painting for thirty thousand years, and you've been watching for millions, determining from a visual scan of a savannah whether it was safe to camp for the night, reading in the eyes of other monkeys whether they could be trusted or not. The image is everything. If you can do it in words in a few seconds, great. If you can do it in pictures with the sound turned off, even better.

"Voters will always tell you they want leaders who are compassionate and articulate, but what they really want is someone they can trust, who is strong and courageous. We are not that removed from our cousins in the trees. When the going gets tough, we want to know if our leader will talk nice to us or defend us."

After it was over, and we had asked all the questions, and Halliwell had answered them with passion and wit, we headed outside for our team-building exercise. Being where we were, Allan had wanted it to be waterskiing, which he learned to do around the time he learned to walk, if you believed the family legend. It would have made for great video, Allan looking nonchalantly determined as he leaned back, smiling, balanced effortlessly, his blond hair flying behind him. But waterskiing is a solitary sport. I convinced Allan to go canoeing instead.

And hidden on the other side of the lake, shooting surreptitiously from behind a screen of trees, was the CTV videographer I had tipped off the week before. On Monday, CTV would run a story on our retreat with exclusive footage of Allan paddling in the same canoe and sharing a joke with a broadly-smiling Jerome Whitchouse, his rival for the leadership. The competition between the two of them during the three-month leadership race had degenerated and given rise to rumours about a major rift in the Party. God knows what the two of them said to each other during the twenty minutes they were out on the water. Allan was of course sitting in the stern. The canoe was almost the exact colour of our Party's logo, and they were both smiling even though they could barely stand to be in the same room together, let alone the same canoe, and the reporter's sound bite would be: "Allan Keyes and his former leadership rival Jerome Whitehouse are shown here paddling in the same direction." By the end of the day after the story aired, any doubts about Party unity were gone, and the pundits had moved on to other things.

MICHAEL

Like most sensible scribes across the country, I thought Allan's decision to run attack ads so soon after assuming the Party leadership was idiotic. My arguments were infinite: he would be sinking to the lowest common denominator, debasing the coin of political discourse and debate, contributing to the ever worsening credibility ratings of politicians, fraying the faith that the average Canadian had in the political process, and breaking the unwritten rule against running attack ads outside of an election cycle.

By slinging the first fistful of radioactive mud, he was asking for more of the same. He was taking the easy way out, wasting the valuable time of Canadians on partisan street fighting when he should have been charting a new course for the twenty-first century. He was going against the grain for most Canadians, who in poll after poll told us they didn't like or listen to negative advertising. [A poll last year by well-known polling firm Public Arena showed that 70 per cent of Canadians did not approve of negative advertising.] He was substituting the negative for the positive, choosing verbal violence over vision.

And like most sensible scribes across our land, except for the smug, worldly commentators who chided the rest of us for being willfully naïve, who lectured us that democratic politics had been ever thus since the golden ages of Athens and Rome, and who advised us we should be thankful we lived in a democratic society where words were the preferred weapon of attack rather than knives or guns or machetes, we ended up being dead wrong.

We all like to think we're better than our neighbours, better than we really are, that we will somehow see through the messages that come our way. Everybody wants to support the small business owned by the person who lives in their community, but we all shop at big box stores because of the better selection and lower prices. The Canadians who looked down on the attack ads nonetheless had their perceptions shaped by them. And Allan and Eli were rewarded. Their strategy was successful, and maybe even more importantly, their strategy was perceived by the majority in Canada to be successful. And when you cut through all the bullshit, through all the aspirations and rhetoric and policy and pretty words, there is nothing more attractive in a politician than the ability to win.

Later, when Allan and Eli came out with their election slogan, "Building a Better Canada," I dismissed it as empty and clichéd and lacking in vision and poetry. It seemed for a brief moment that Eli had lost his touch. But the platform the Party put forward for Allan to run on resonated with most Canadians. It was simple and clear, with an emphasis on three major areas: post-secondary education, the environment, and the economy.

They promised more federal funding for universities to improve research, teaching, and student bursaries. In a bold but smart move, they proposed carbon regulations on industry, which sent a message to the public that they would be tough on climate change without appearing to place a burden on individual consumers and taxpayers. They also proposed more stringent air emission regulations and new legislation to protect fresh water, which they recognized would be the next great global environmental cause, after climate change. They proposed a series of economic measures designed to streamline regulations for new businesses and infrastructure projects, take the lowest income earners off the tax rolls, reduce taxes for small businesses, and extend the accelerated capital cost allowance for manufacturers to deduct investments in plant equipment. And they committed to a national focus on supporting

Canadian industry leaders in five key areas: banking, natural resources and energy, information technology, manufacturing, and aerospace.

They also had smaller and inexpensive but attractively positioned fiscal programs designed to appeal directly to key slices of the electorate, in the areas of arts and culture, children's sports, and seniors. All in all, the platform promised common sense, pragmatism, and results over any grand vision that might look great on paper but would be impossible to implement in real life. It had Eli's fingerprints on every page: it was steady, smart, and perfectly aligned with the mood of the public.

Throughout the campaign, Allan and Eli stayed away from the grand vision, from conventional ideas of rhetoric. They knew that Canadians like their leaders to be capable of handling themselves behind a podium, but not to be such smooth or skilled speakers that they come across as insincere. Like the Americans, and unlike the Europeans, we don't like our leaders to be too articulate. Allan would always be a master of words, but I noticed that in his first campaign as leader, and as the years went on, he learned to calibrate his vocabulary and syntax, avoiding complex words and phrases that sounded too intellectual, in favour of simple words and simple constructions. By the time he became Prime Minister, he and Eli would know that we choose our leaders not because of what they say, but because of who they are.

ELI

Although Allan never really felt comfortable with them, the attack ads served their purpose. They allowed us to take the initiative. They bought us the time and space we needed to define ourselves. They were our flawless opening.

Like every political party promising sweeping change and committed to forging ahead into the future, we reached back into our past for experience and inspiration. We made the requisite head-hunter telephone calls, hosted the long courtship lunches where everyone put their naked dreams on the table, and successfully wooed back from exile in Toronto and Montreal a core group of the strategists and advisers who had served loyally under Laffrey before being cast out when the regime changed.

After departing, most of Laffrey's inner circle had moved seamlessly into the support and dependency industries that survive on the edges of politics: lobbying, public relations, research and polling, and the safe haven of the law firms. Some of these people were coy when we first approached them, hiding their desire to return to Ottawa because they were naturally stoics or good negotiators, but most could hardly wait to come back. Once you have worked on Parliament Hill, the virus never leaves your body.

We rehabilitated Don Melrose, Laffrey's former chief of staff and, because we were preparing for a war, we also brought back Laffrey's war room director, Andrew Compton. We were very lucky that Compton agreed to re-enter the Ottawa fray. Compton appreciated that while politics and sports might be the more sophisticated, cultured, and well-spoken grandchildren of war, they have the same objective: to win by destroying your opponent, burning his villages, sowing his fields with salt, taking his farms and livestock. Of course we cover it up with talk of excellence and patriotism and skill and beauty. We toast the victorious generals in their dress uniforms at balls, we pin medals and ribbons on their chests, and genuflect at the altar of their victories, but the spirit and the process are the same.

The BlackBerry was our Gatling gun in the political war, game-changing in how we took territory and attacked the enemy in an election process that had previously been static by comparison. It seemed like we had always had our BlackBerrys. But we were only one election removed from a time when you couldn't email reporters with the facts before your opponent had finished his speech. It was war in its best, oldest sense, all about disrupting the enemy, his lines of communications, his bunkers of reason, his ability to think, distracting him with salvos and ambushes, keeping him on the run so that he made mistakes. Andrew was one of the first people in Canada to truly understand the potential of the BlackBerry and apply it to politics.

Andrew was a poli-sci professor, but he was as comfortable off-campus as he was among his journals. He had written his dissertation on technology and communications and had published articles on political strategy and the emergent social media. Heading up Laffrey's war room in his last election was what Andrew did for sport and relaxation. It was what he did for fun, the way other men golf or tinker with cars. In the weeks leading up to and during our election, he gleefully buried himself in a bunker where posters blanked out every window and where college kids, whose eyes burned with the true devotion of the fanatic, stared for twenty hours at a time at TV and computer screens, and screamed on cell phones, and knelt in prayer over BlackBerrys, and compressed the time of our fathers and grandfathers into bite-sized slices so that journalists received our story while our opponents were still stumbling through their speeches on old-fashioned podiums.

With that tour of duty, a national reputation would be bestowed on Andrew that framed him as a hyper-partisan, vicious political thug, an opportunistic tactician who couldn't think big or see past a sound bite, and as a show-off. I never understood where his public persona came from because anyone who actually spent five minutes with him came away convinced that he was one of the gentlest people they had ever met: thoughtful, soft-spoken, self-effacing. The kind of person who, if he found a spider in his home, couldn't bring himself to kill it but would trap it carefully in his hands and relocate it outside.

Andrew was also like one of those drug dealers who never used what he sold. He thrived in a world where multi-tasking was an understatement, and he managed a constant interpretation and flow of information in which people wrote with their thumbs and screens flashed, but he never indulged in his heady brand of information crack. He himself never multi-tasked, because he felt there was no such thing. In his view, you were either concentrating on one thing at a time or else you were doing a lot of things but none of them well. Most surprising for me, he didn't have a TV at home or at work. He believed the twenty-four-hour news cycle had become far too distracting and corrupted his ability to think strategically and take a long-term view. In this way, he was also a bit like one of those great actors who never watches any of his own films.

One of the most memorable scenes in one of my favourite movies, Clint Eastwood's Western *Unforgiven*, is when Eastwood's character walks into a bar. The set piece has been foreshadowed earlier in the film when Eastwood tells someone that it's a lot harder to shoot a man than it looks, not morally but physically, and that most people panic when they're holding a gun. Eastwood explains there's another man in front of them, and they don't take their time because they're worried they're going to get shot themselves. So they start firing, barely taking time to aim, and as a result they usually get shot themselves. It sounds interesting, but it's shown well later in the film. By the time you've forgotten all about Eastwood's mini-lecture on time, his character swings through the saloon doors. Inside are about thirty men, all of who want to kill him. He makes some noise as he walks in, pushing the doors in front of him. For a second there's silence, then all the men pull their guns and start firing, wildly, passionately, hurriedly. And Eastwood's cowboy takes his time, doesn't work up a sweat, picks them off one by one, squeezing the trigger patiently. And it's the movies, so he shoots them all, and he's unscathed, but still he's made his point.

After having served with Allan in Ottawa for over a decade and a half, I came to realize a lot of things, but perhaps the biggest lesson for me was that success is often a function of time. Governments, companies, individuals make many mistakes. Some are minor. Most are ones nobody ever hears of. Others bring down governments or destroy careers. If an organization has good processes, it might do a post mortem. But even with the best processes it will often misdiagnose. It will blame every possible culprit – faulty planning, poor execution, bad communication (my favourite, the eternal scapegoat), misalignment, a lack of prioritization, insufficient resources, events outside of their control (what we fashionably call black swans), the list goes on and on – but often miss the cause, because it's too obvious, too simple. The cause is time. I've been part of too many meetings and too many decisions to think that people usually fail because they're stupid or inexperienced. There's enough of that to go around, but in almost every case they fail because they don't have enough time and because they often compound the problem by misusing what little time they have.

I would like to say that we won our first election with Allan as leader, but as is so often the case in politics, the other side lost. During the campaign it became clear that the incumbent PM had worn out his welcome, alienated too many constituencies after two terms. He made that mistake which is unfortunately so common in politicians and professional athletes – he had become overconfident in his competence, thought he was invincible. Like an old athlete with a bad sense of timing, he stayed on too long, after his skills and reflexes and instincts had already begun to degrade.

We rode to power on the oldest of political waves, the first chapter in every how-to-get-elected handbook: the desire for change. And we still had relative youth on our side. Truth be told, this was supposed to be a liability when Allan ran for the leadership but was seen as a plus three years later when Allan ran to be PM. Allan was a great candidate at forty. The older men in the party expected Allan to be Leader of the Opposition for three years and lose the next election; then it would be their turn to contend. They saw Allan as the sacrificial lamb, but instead he seized the moment. And like Napoleon, who believed that the bold man created his own luck, Allan was in the right place at the right time, when public sentiment shifted.

Like all winners, we also got lucky in a tactical sense. In the months leading up to the election, two Cabinet ministers had to resign when accusations surfaced about them having accepted gifts and trips from a European manufacturer of armored vehicles that was lobbying them. In the end, after a two-year police investigation and public inquiry that the former PM had called for, the two were acquitted. They had committed one or two venial sins but were mostly pure in the eyes of the law. However, by then everything had changed. Their government was out of office, and their reputations would never be the same.

In the final weeks of the campaign, we continued to climb in the polls, creating our own momentum, writing our own story. The editors of the major papers endorsed our platform and the unarticulated but golden promise that Allan could rise above regional factionalism and unite the country behind him. We were being careful not to peak too soon or appear over-confident, but Allan was unobtrusively appearing prime ministerial whenever he spoke and wherever he appeared, and we were neatly avoiding risks when we made nearly the last mistake of the campaign. I was reminded of Michael's grandmaster dictum that the winner in chess is the one who makes the second-to-last mistake. Like a chess game, every election is a collection of not necessarily brilliant moves but rather an exchange of mistakes that the other side takes turns exploiting until finally one side takes advantage of the last mistake and becomes the winner.

Allan was speaking at the opening of a new senior citizens' home in southern Ontario. He was charming everyone, whether they had Alzheimer's or not, smiling and joking like everybody's most adored son or grandson, when he was casually asked by one of the national reporters who was along for the ride if he would raise taxes if he were to be elected. There are some questions that every politician learns early on never to answer, because there is no way to win and because telling the truth is a sure way to lose. Any question about taxes falls into that category of the unanswerable. You acknowledge the question if you are polite, and then you move on to something else. Everyone goes along with it, because it's part of the game. But for some reason, that day Allan didn't play along. Maybe it was because he was tired, or maybe his guard was down because he was with people who were losing their minds. Perhaps he felt he was in a position where he could tell Canadians what they needed to hear, or maybe he was concerned about recent rounds of tax cuts and he wanted to do the right thing. Whatever the reason, Allan said, "As a result of the tax cuts in recent years, I think everyone recognizes that any government that is committed to continuing to fund the Canada we all value will have to raise taxes in a small way."

The reporters smiled, paid heed to their BlackBerrys, and performed their stand-ups in front of the cameras outside. Within hours, we were being pilloried and spun by the Government as old-time taxers and spenders, reckless with taxpayers' money, conspiring to make government larger and inefficient. The other parties piled on, and the media reported their criticisms as gospel. We were being punished for telling the truth, and the old bogeyman was back: Allan was a rich man's son out of touch with the average Canadian. We could have lost the election but the Government made the last mistake of the campaign by going over the top and getting personal. So although Allan's comment hurt us, the extreme tone of the Government's attacks on their young and telegenic opponent weakened the thrust of their criticism. After having enjoyed a comfortable lead for most of the campaign, we ended up winning a majority on May 25, 2005 by a narrow margin of seven seats.

SOPHIE

Katherine and I didn't spend any real time together until a month after Allan was elected PM. We'd seen each other on election night, but it wasn't until the next meeting of our book club that we were able to sit down and talk. It was a small book club: Katherine and I; Linda McIntyre, a psychology professor at Carleton; Savannah Laskey, a civil rights lawyer; and Geneviève Lafrance, a curator at the Museum of Civilization. Other than Katherine and I, everyone was originally from Ottawa. But Katherine was an exception in another sense. While the rest of us picked novels or short story collections we liked or admired, the books Katherine always chose to make us read were non-fiction. I never said anything, but I was most unimpressed when Katherine picked one of Michael's books: *Life After NAFTA*. (Although, to be fair to her, as far as I could tell nobody had ever told her anything about Michael, Eli, and me.)

I don't remember much of the book; I gave up after Michael's first couple of footnote-laden chapters. But ever since then I always had a soft spot for NAFTA. This was because seeing Michael's photo on the book jacket reminded me of the night I met Eli. Michael looked older in his photo, as Eli did by that time, but both of them still looked a lot like the boys they'd been in university. The photo had reminded me of everything that had changed and stayed the same. When I first met Eli, at that McGill party, I liked him. The way he looked, the sound of his voice, the cute and pathetic way he tried so hard to impress me by taking me to some crazy poetry reading and then writing me poems. As if that would impress me. But it did. I just never told him. I didn't want him to become a poet for me. I wasn't sure I wanted to be married to a poet, his parents' great monogamous love affair notwithstanding. And I didn't want him to think I was easily impressed.

I did feel badly about Michael. We were never really going out, but he was the one who brought me to that party. I found out later from Eli that Michael hardly ever went to parties, so I guess he thought I liked them. I might never have met Eli if it weren't for Michael. I knew they had been close. I knew it from what Michael told me about Eli on the way to the party. Michael was really looking forward to introducing me to Eli. In those fifteen minutes he told me all about him, about their chess games, their fathers, their dreams of being writers. After Eli and I were together for a while, despite my coolness to his poems, I thought I was marrying a poet, or at least some kind of writer. Maybe a teacher. A professor, if he could stay focused. I never thought he'd end up doing what he did. I know he didn't. I never thought we'd move to Ottawa. I never thought he'd spend so much time at the office, waking up so early to read the news, staying up so late to watch it.

I knew we would have children together, but never knew how much they would make me ache, the smell of their skin, their hair, like little animals. I never knew conceiving children would be so easy. Didn't know at first how so many people had so much trouble, and had to go to doctors and test their sperm and eggs and get fertility treatments and pray and have sex in certain ways and eat certain foods and give up running and try in-vitro. With us it was too easy. I'd go off the pill or we'd stop using condoms and fall into bed and a few weeks later there I would be, vomiting up my guts. I could have had ten more, and sometimes I wish we had.

Eli took this easy fertility of ours for granted, too. So different from Katherine and Allan's experience. Katherine had shared with me that conceiving their two sons, Max and Marc, had not been easy. As far as I knew, Allan had never mentioned this once to Eli.

152

We were at Linda's house in South Ottawa, just a few blocks from where she taught. Linda's husband, also a professor at Carleton, was putting their children to bed, and for the first half hour, our conversation was competing with laughter and running footsteps upstairs. Men and women approach their children's bedtime rituals so differently. I always worried about proper toothbrushing and face-washing. Eli preferred to chase and wrestle our children into their beds.

Every one of us in book club enjoyed our reading, but our group wasn't overly structured. We never followed or prepared answers to the discussion questions you find at the end of some books that make you feel you're back in high school. We talked as much about ourselves as the books. And there was always one among us who hadn't managed to finish the book in time, either because she was too busy at work or home or because she'd found it boring. Four weeks after one of our members had helped to elect a prime minister, our collective focus on our book was less acute than usual. We didn't just congratulate Katherine on Allan's victory. We all knew the role she had played, and we proudly toasted her achievement.

In between discussing Alice Munro's short story collection *Runaway*, which had won the Giller Prize the year before, drinking too many glasses of red wine, and savouring biscotti from La Bottega, everyone asked Katherine the questions we had been saving up since election night. What is 24 Sussex Drive like? Nice. Is it true you are always accompanied by an RCMP security detail? Yes, look outside. Two of us got up to look. And there it was: the dark sedan, the two officers' watchful poses. Are you worried about the safety of your children? Of them growing up in a bubble? Of course, but you have to trust the system and yourselves. Do you enjoy having domestic help? In a way, but it's strange hardly ever being alone. Are Allan's days really long, and is he tired all the time? Yes, and mostly. But not all the time.

After we had tried to explain for each other's benefit Munro's deceptively simple genius, Linda asked Katherine what she was most concerned about in Allan's victory. Katherine deliberately didn't look at me as she put down her glass and replied, "I know we won and we're two years past the attack ads, but I still worry about their effect on Allan's legacy, when all is said and done. And written."

I knew Katherine had resented Eli for his recommendation to run attack ads. And no doubt Allan for accepting it. But she took another bite of biscotti and sip of wine, and without looking at anyone in particular, as if she were thinking aloud, said slowly, "But that's a minor concern. More and more I find myself wondering about the economy. I mean things look okay, but our productivity and innovation are not where they should be. The strength of our dollar is exposing those weaknesses. Our industries have been coasting along, not making the necessary investments. And I know I'm in a minority here, and it's just a feeling, but I worry about the US. Right now their economy is strong, but it's never good to be so dependent on one market."

I'd never been overly interested in economics, and so I asked Katherine what she was least worried about. She relaxed her shoulders and leaned back. "If I'm most worried about the numbers, I'm least worried about the words. You know I provided Eli with the content for the economic section of Allan's acceptance speech. But when I was listening to Allan speak, it was like I was hearing everything for the first time. It reminded me of a poem, the way they used to teach us about poetry in high school, remember? Every word the right one, every one in its place, no extras." Katherine had attended Trafalgar, the private girls' school at the foot of Mount Royal. As a high school student wearing jeans to public school, I used to secretly envy the private school girls with their crisp shirts and their kilts.

Katherine shook her head and laughed. "It's always amazing,

really – I never get used to hearing Allan speak when he can barely write a grammatical paragraph. He even trips himself up when he writes the boys birthday cards. He never remembers if he's writing English or French or Italian. He mixes up the syntax and the idioms. Thank God for Eli." She wagged her finger at me. "Although he always refuses to ever take any credit, as you know."

I knew.

"'It's all Allan, I just correct his mental punctuation.'" And we all burst out laughing, because Katherine had delivered that last line in a pitch-perfect rendition of how Eli spoke, with his deep voice and serious tone. He rarely told jokes in public, because he was afraid they might be misinterpreted. Katherine had made her imitation sound both sincere and ridiculous at the same time.

"I wonder if Eli will change his answer when he's over for supper at 24 Sussex Drive," Geneviève said, and we all laughed again.

MICHAEL

Everything went well for Allan and Eli at the start of their mandate. Their political honeymoon lasted a full twelve months, a geological era in politics, before they were cross-checked head-first into the boards with their first scandal. As political scandals go in Canada, we barely register on the world stage. We're Amish children in a world of drug dealing, swinging adults. Our scandals never come close to British ones, with their mélange of ancient class undertones and modern-day dominatrixes, or to the adolescent exhibitionism of American scandals, with their comic book captain-of-the-football-team-doing-unmentionable-things-with-the-cheerleader subtexts. [Think Profumo politically keeling over after Christine Keeler in Britain, and Bill Clinton's struggles with interns and semantics in DC.]

We often use the signposts of elections to make sense of politics, to frame it, measure it, and declare the winners and losers, just as we rely on statuettes at the Oscars or points in football games. But the true metronome of political life in a democracy is scandal. It's the spice we use to liven up the bland servings of our political meal. Scandal's also our drama, our catharsis. It meets our need to spill blood on the floor and to see it spilled. We like to see the mighty fall, and to see the sand thrown down to soak up the blood. So we return to our roots in Athens and Rome and to a story that is infinitely more real to us than dry dissertations on budgets and taxes and legislative reform. To have a good scandal, you need one of two things: sex or money (or its surrogate), either in overabundance or deviation. And you usually, although not always, need a male politician. In Canada our scandals are almost always about money. But Allan's government was about to experience the exception that proves the rule.

Jerome Whitehouse was a political recruiter's wet dream before he succumbed to the siren call of politics. He was an accomplished, telegenic, articulate, wealthy, bilingual corporate lawyer with longish – by politicians' standards – flowing hair, a bright smile that belonged more to a movie star than a Canadian legislator, a deep, distinctive voice that sounded beautiful on radio, and what all of us, for lack of a better name, call charisma. Whitehouse had the wattage level of charisma that caused many outside his party, including yours truly, and even some inside it, to assume he would be leader some day. He came very close to defeating Allan in the leadership race, and although he happened to say all the right things afterwards, going out of his way to affirm, confirm, and reaffirm his undying loyalty to Allan at every opportunity, he managed to do so in a way that somehow suggested he himself would have been a better choice for leader.

Whitehouse was one of those politicians who regularly appeared in the political society columns, his name and photo running more often under the "hot" than the "not" heading, usually alongside his latest "friend," as we in the media so politely termed the woman who happened to be clinging to his arm on any particular night: at hockey games, rock concerts, charity fundraisers, political gatherings. It was part of his personal brand, his political image, youthful, fresh, fun: the rock star as politician.

When his political career imploded, he was Minister of Foreign Affairs, jetting around the world, spreading our influence, soft power, international message, whatever the Government happened to call it then, and charming the pants and the skirts off everyone. And like many shooting stars in the political firmament, he was brought to his knees by the modern politician's kryptonite: a picture. The day after a photograph of Whitehouse appeared with his latest girlfriend, taking in Pat Metheny at the Jazz Festival in Montreal, the two of them glowing almost radioactively in a crowd of a hundred thousand, the news director at a local radio station in Moose Jaw was catching up on the TV news when he thought he recognized the woman in the photo. He turned on his laptop, went to one of his most-frequented web sites, and confirmed his suspicion.

The next day, his station broke the story that Whitehouse's latest girlfriend had a very public secret identity. She had a webcam set up in her bedroom, with rather predictable results for her regular viewers. Within hours, all of us were chasing the story from coast to coast. It was a perfect political story: "High-profile politician found in bed of web bedroom star." It was like Christmas in July for tabloid headline writers: "Domestic Affairs undo Foreign Minister," "New use for bedroom in Whitehouse," "Webcamgate," "House on fire," "Whitehouse unplugged and unzipped." In the beginning, the story was pure fun, all about stupidity, humiliation, and sex. But after forty-eight hours, like a fire following the oxygen, the story shifted to national security and the risks that Whitehouse was exposing the nation to when he decided to sleep with a woman who had a webcam trained on her antique mahogany four-poster bed. I am proud to say *The Mail and Post* led the charge on this more serious angle.

The Government's communications strategy was obvious: Whitehouse would maintain a dignified silence as he went about his public business, a solemn expression on his face whenever a camera pointed in his direction, as if the whole sordid issue were purely personal and beneath his attention as a Minister of the Crown. Eli would speak for the Government and the Prime Minister.

ELI

Half an hour after we spoke with Whitehouse, I was doing the scrum down on the first floor of Centre Block. I felt like several generations of good peasant stock in a very long Hundred Years' War, smiling politely while taking direct fire in the face. I was way out in front, taking bullets in my thick skin, keeping my cool. With a shrug and a smile, I was absorbing the sarcasm and disbelief of the media, dodging everything being thrown at me like mental judo, where you move more than you punch or kick and you use your opponent's strength against him.

In chess, white always goes first. It's the most important first-move advantage in any game, and it's far more important than the coin toss in football. Playing white is comparable to being the one who launches the first intercontinental ballistic strike. Everything else is catch-up. The advantage that first-move status confers in chess, assuming the players are evenly matched, is so great that when grandmasters play black, their objective for the game is no longer to win but to fight for the impressive honour of a stalemate or a draw.

In the media there is the same first move advantage. We are complicated mammals. Only ten thousand years out of the cave, we compose symphonies and write poetry, crack atoms and build bombs that Genghis Khan could only dream of in his most seductive nightmares. We operate remotely on people's organs with robots. But we are still hardwired like our ancestors. They had to make successful judgments about threats and opportunities – in the form of tusks and clubs and spears – in less than a second. And it was only the genes of our successful ancestors that survived.

We make up our minds – about the characters, who's right, who's wrong, about the plot, the theme, the conclusion – the first time we hear or read or see a story. Every subsequent story in that book, or every new installment if it's in serial form, no matter how much more nuanced or edited, revised, or even different, is seen through the original paradigm. It's the same with people. Research on the process and practice of job interviews has shown that prospective employers make up their minds within about thirty seconds of sitting down across from the person they are interviewing. Every subsequent question is asked and every subsequent answer is interpreted within the original bias of whether to hire or not. The stakes are higher, but the human thought process is the same when it comes to those high profile media stories about criminal charges that result in a not-guilty verdict.

On the first day, the accused is splayed across the front page, being led away, usually caught looking sullen and surprised, or in some cases serene or defiant. Months later, during the trial, more of the story, sometimes what passes for the "full story," will slowly emerge. Perhaps years later, if the person is innocent, there will be a small story on the inside pages. But for most people, who have many other things to think about, like whether their husband or wife really loves them or whether they will be able to pay their mortgage, that person will be forever guilty, as they were on the first day. After that, time stands still.

If you are not the one controlling the story, what information is released, when, by whom, in what order, and at what pace and frequency, you are playing black in a chess game. You are reacting to events, to your opponents, to the rules and rhythms of the media.

We were reacting, and we were fighting not for victory but for a draw. We had three messages to convey: Jerome had never taken any confidential briefing documents out of Cabinet and certainly had never taken any to his girlfriend's house; the government had

160

no place in the bedroom of the nation, whether it was webcam-equipped or not; and Jerome had never been filmed with the web-cam. It had been turned off every time he visited.

We took our lumps, the cartoonists had even more fun with Jerome than the headline writers, and it was a two-day story. Jerome clipped the best cartoons and, good sport that he was, sent them out to be framed for his office. Everyone clapped me on the back, and we had a few beers. One week later, a photo of a fully unclothed Jerome started to make the rounds on the web. It had been taken by webcam girl. When we met with Jerome, he claimed the photo had been taken without his knowledge, but he understood the rules of the game. He had his resignation ready. Allan thanked him for his service, somehow managed not to smile in his presence, and accepted his resignation. I had to do a few interviews, and we all appeared with serious expressions in front of the cameras for the rest of the week. A major rival to Allan had tripped on his own sword, *double entendre* intended, and the Government sailed on.

MICHAEL

One morning, my mother called me at the office to tell me she was leaving my father. If you've ever worked in a newsroom, you know they aren't designed for private conversations. You sit practically on top of each other like chickens in one of those trucks bound for the slaughterhouse. If you're used to working in an office, sitting in the openness of a newsroom is like joining a nudist colony. You're self-conscious at first, but then you lose all your inhibitions and just go with the flow.

You hear everyone's phone ringing and at least half of every conversation. You have a close-up view of how people's behaviour deteriorates over the course of the day. You and your colleagues slip from the early morning, when you drink coffee, tell one another jokes, talk about the news, to the middle of the day. By then, everyone's chasing down a multi-stranded story, headsets on, fingers flying over their keyboards. At the end of the day, when deadline is closing in, you're all rushing to wrestle competing points of view, facts, and versions of the world into a coherent, articulate, compelling piece that can be quickly understood by tomorrow's reader. By this point you no longer have time for complete sentences outside of your story. Newsrooms are like trading floors for people who were never very good with numbers. You can smell one another's mental sweat. If you're lucky, you get a buzz out of it.

When my mother called, at 2.37 pm on a Monday, the whole room stopped its usual mad spinning and went still and quiet for me. I was a little boy again, inarticulate, shy, just learning to make sense of the ways of the adult world. What do you say to a woman who's just turned sixty-five and who's called to tell you she's decided to leave your father after forty years of marriage and at least one affair? My mother obviously felt the need to call me with the news because I hadn't been back to Montreal for a few months. She could have waited until I got home, but she liked to do things on her own time.

She was very calm and matter of fact, like a schoolteacher explaining the meaning of a painting to an eight-year-old. She gave the impression of having rehearsed her short speech, because her words had a logical, unemotional flow. There were no "ums" or "ahs" or awkward silences as she struggled to find a word, and she neatly pre-empted any initial questions I might have had.

After a quick hello, she jumped right to the point. "I've decided to leave your father. I've spoken with him about it a few times over the course of the past month. He'll be fine. We should have done it years ago. I've already picked out an apartment. It's just three blocks away on Beaconsfield above Sherbrooke, so there won't be much of a change for me there. Money won't be a problem either. It's all looked after. I wanted you to be the first to know."

Silence for a while. I think she knew what was coming. I was not sure if I would be able to say the words. I could, but just barely. "You know…that I knew about you…and…." I remembered that I never knew his name. I never wanted to know. I didn't want to know at that moment.

"I didn't know at first. But after a while I figured it out. You stopped looking at me the same way." A pause. "You were never very good at dissembling."

"And I never forgave myself for not telling Dad."

She didn't thank me because she knew I didn't do it for her. All she said was, "I know."

I couldn't believe we were having this conversation then – I was 43 years old – and in the newsroom. I knew I should have said I would call her back later when I was at home, or at least have gone to one of those tiny depressing rooms the size of a phone booth that organizations provide for people without offices to make private calls, but I didn't care. "I've never asked you this…." I paused for a few seconds, not sure again if I would be able to speak. "But why did you do it?" I didn't have to ask why my parents stayed together. Even though my father had never said, I had known forever that he stayed for me.

"Have the affair." It was not a question.

"Yeah."

"Does there always have to be a reason? Do you think everything always has a reason behind it? My son the Vulcan wordsmith." A tight laugh. "Do you think everything can always be expressed in words?"

"Yes."

"I could ask you why you gave up chess or stopped being friends with Eli." I didn't bother telling her those examples hurt her argument. I might not have had the best reasons but I did have reasons. But she didn't wait for a response. "I don't know. Maybe I was bored, but that's a boring answer. Twenty-five years later I'm still not sure."

People around me were trying to concentrate, but my conversation had pulled them away from their deadlines, and they were listening and looking at me while trying not to. I still didn't care. I was interviewing my mother. Asking questions. Drawing conclusions. Trying to make sense of things. It's what I had done most of my life.

"That's it? After all this time you don't have a better answer." I found I was speaking more easily again but I sounded angry. I didn't like to sound angry.

"No. I'm sorry, Michael. Not everything in my world has an answer."

We were about to end the call when I asked my last question.

"Why now?"

Silence for a few seconds. A good interviewee organizing her thoughts. "There was no big epiphany. As I said, I should have done it a long time ago. Maybe he should have left me. We tried to work things out. At first it was for you, then it was for us. Then it was because we had tried for so long."

I put down the phone, and went back to the story I was writing on Canada's sluggish progress in tackling the productivity issue, compared to many of the economies in the developing world.

ELI

Sophie took me to Rome in 2006 for my fortieth birthday. I had actually turned forty the year before, but we had postponed the trip because Allan has just been elected PM. After our third child was born, Sophie had stopped working full-time, but she withdrew a few thousand dollars from her savings account and bought us tickets. I had always wanted to go, and we had always planned to, but there was always work, and then there were kids, and we had never gotten around to it.

We did the usual touristy things: the ruined Forum, the Trevi Fountain, the Vatican, the Coliseum with its present-day Romans dressed up as legionaries and gladiators for the amusement of the modern Visigoths. We braved the hyper crowds from every country who were so busy taking perfect pictures with their digital cameras to bore their family and friends with back home that, without ever being aware of it, they were skipping right over the experience to the memories. Sophie even stood by and let me piss on the Arch of Titus.

When I first mentioned it, she thought I was joking, so I told her the story. Titus and his father, Emperor Vespasian, suppressed the Jewish rebellion and reconquered Jerusalem in 70 AD like good, efficient Romans. But two thousand Jews had inconveniently held out in Herod's palace fortress at the top of Masada. One of Titus's generals camped out in the desert and besieged Masada for two years, only to be denied the great prize when he finally gained entry and discovered the bodies of almost all the inhabitants, who had taken their own lives rather than become slaves to the Romans.

It had been something of a cult tradition ever since for Jews visiting Rome to bestow upon the Arch of Titus an arc of urine, and in so doing make an eloquent comment about Roman civilization having long crumbled, despite brilliantly designed siege engines and well-trained legions and the habit of crucifixion, while the Jews were still alive and kicking two thousand years later. When Sophie realized I was serious, she tried to talk me out of it by convincing me public urination was barbaric and unhygienic, and that times had changed in the decades since my father had visited Rome. In the end, when all her arguments were breaking into pieces on the edges of my smile, she just shook her head and looked the other way as I unzipped my pants.

I had brought along my university copy of Juvenal's *Satires* and I read his gloriously splenetic verses to Sophie each night before bed, both of us happily shocked at how modern Juvenal and Rome sounded to our twenty-first century ears. We walked the winding streets and threw coins into the fountains, we ate and drank outdoors, and we made love indoors and once quietly at night on the balcony. We thought the thoughts that tourists think in Rome. The rise and fall of empires. Civilization's thin veneer like a layer of marble covering the rough stone underneath. The fragility of a society that, despite its ornate laws and customs, still fears the barbarians outside the gates. Its toleration, if not celebration, of the barbarism within, the current age's version of gladiators and vestal virgins, and inbred emperors murdering each other. While thousands of miles away, on some steppes off the edge of the map, hungrier, hairier, less educated men sharpen their swords and dream about conquest.

I would like to say that I made my fortieth birthday trip vow while exploring Rome's marvelous marble ruins – it would have been more fitting – and I could probably get away with it because nobody else would know, but the truth is I made my vow while boarding the plane in London after we connected from Rome. We had a couple of hours to spare at Heathrow, and I found my way to my usual destination in any airport: the bookstore. In the non-fiction bestseller section, prominently displayed, I couldn't miss twenty-five hardcover copies of Michael's latest in a long line of international political bestsellers: *Lion in Ottawa: The Laffrey Years.* It was a testament to Michael's skill that he was able to make the politics and politicians of a middle power relevant around the world. I didn't buy the book – I didn't even take a copy down and flip the pages – but I stared at it for a long time.

I didn't say anything to Sophie as we boarded and took our seats – she had splurged on first class – but I closed my eyes tightly for ten seconds while fastening my seatbelt, and I made a vow to myself. I had turned forty-one the night before.

MICHAEL

As the years went by, and time started speeding up, as the years started to feel like months, and the weeks like days, I never stopped being professionally impressed by how Allan used words. He was a throwback to those days when politicians valued oratory, when words meant something, when it wasn't all about shouting out your opponent in Question Period and getting sound bites right for a bright nine-second TV burst. There was something about the way he spoke in complete sentences, almost old-fashioned. Unfashionable. Un-hip. Un-modern. When Allan went "iambic," to appropriate a phrase from that American word warrior Pat Buchanan, he was very un-MTV. And still he looked good on TV and he was cool. He was, in the adolescent lingo of our time, authentic.

When he did an interview, you didn't feel he was feeding you pre-cut, pre-washed, pre-approved statements that some second-rate PR flack had composed for him. You could see the wheels turning in his head as he reflected on the question. He didn't bother condensing his thoughts into easily digestible bits of pablum for the masses. He was not afraid to think on his feet. Not afraid to shrug and admit he didn't know the answer. Now that he'd reached the pinnacle, he didn't ever take the time to respond to the attacks of his enemies with more attacks. He just smiled and listened and thought clearly and spoke eloquently. He was the anti-modern political communications idol.

As far as I could tell, although I knew he had, he didn't appear to have ever worked off a written speech in nearly twenty years in political life. He had a few key ideas, and obviously practised and

169

refined his points, his examples, his sentences, his rhythm. But every word appeared unrehearsed and sincere. And he never seemed to give the same speech twice. Each time it appeared new, unique, created completely for the benefit of that specific audience, whether it was cocky Bay Streeters eager for new markets to safely park their clients' flighty capital, or high school students trying to navigate the world from the supportive launching pad of a small town. He should have been destroyed like a naked Christian facing a lion in the modern media arena that idolized sound bites expressed in nine seconds over complex thoughts. The beast had no tolerance for long-winded answers, no sympathy for subtlety or equivocation. And yet Allan kept going, as popular twenty years in as he was at the beginning, winning election after election, beating away challenger after challenger.

As trust in politicians reached depressingly low levels in the new millennium, comparable to the trust in us flacks and the lawyers that most federal politicians still were, Allan remained unscathed and untouchable. [In most surveys about trust, politicians are dead last. Journalists are usually one or sometimes two places above them. I don't think it's a coincidence that both work predominantly with words.] And behind him, working with his natural style, letting him flout all the conventions, and supporting him like a quiet cornerman in the boxing ring, was Eli.

Eli had a gift. He had many gifts, but perhaps his most valuable one was that he could get out the news he wanted and kill the news he didn't want. Not kill it by hiding it, but by making the news he wanted to keep under wraps appear inconsequential in relation to everything else. He left reporters, and more importantly the public, with the impression that what he didn't want them to focus on wasn't worth exploring or even worth knowing. He was like a minor deity of his chosen medium, who could turn on the sun or the rain and turn it off again at will, despite all the efforts of us lesser mortals to stop his mastery of weather or even to catch him in the act.

It helped that he was affable and that he never lost his cool, no matter how much people tempted or provoked him. People had tried. He was never rude, and he never swore, at least not on the job – not even the slightest "fuck" silently mouthed when things went wrong. [In this respect, the little Tredman apple fell fucking far from the tree.] And he never gave a straight "No," regardless of what news he had to deliver. He could speak for hours about politics, about the weather, about your family, and come across as sincere, nice, smart, and interested in you, without ever giving anything away. His old-fashioned demeanor suited the style of his boss. He was almost courtly in the serious, respectful way he greeted you, whether you were there to take notes and obediently transcribe the story that the PMO wanted you to run, or even if your only mission that day was to embarrass and humiliate the Government. He was proof that you could say a lot of things when you said them with a smile.

When you spoke, he just listened in a way that people hardly ever listened any more. Most were just waiting to get their word in and hear themselves, and didn't look you in the eyes when they did speak. He shut out all distractions and made you feel you were the most important person in the room, or even the world. We didn't speak a lot or for long, but we'd see each other at some of the same cocktail parties and many of the same news conferences, and I would watch him. In meetings, he only stepped out to take the PM's calls, and he always did this with a shrug, a quietly expressed and embarrassed apology. We all understood. We didn't hold it against him. When he was at a political or business function, and the room was swimming with rich and powerful people whose opinions mattered and whose perception of you could be set for life on the basis of a well-timed smile or an opening comment, he never gave you the impression that he was marking time with you.

His eyes didn't dart around the room looking for someone else with more wealth or power.

As I think about it now, maybe Eli's most invaluable professional quality was his empathy, honed no doubt through all his literary reading. How can you hope to convince people you're right if you have no idea what's going on inside their hearts and minds? My dad didn't have to worry about this when he was teaching English, writing articles, and trying to write a biography of Adam Tredman. However, as universities started to have less money to go around in the fiscally conservative and Hobbesian late eighties and nineties, especially for faculties that didn't lead students by the hand to the promised land of a well-paying job, literature faculties had to come up with arguments to justify their existence.

They used to love to say they taught unformed undergrads how to be critical thinkers. Canadian banker Matthew Barrett even said that he'd rather hire literature majors than accountants because you could teach someone how to read a balance sheet in a day but anybody who could read and interpret Chaucer obviously knew how to think. But the literary academy committed an existential faux pas when they traipsed down the primrose path of literary theory. (Fuck, how I hated Foucault.) It would take psychology, another soft discipline, to figure out that reading made-up stories about imaginary people and putting yourselves in their figurative shoes would probably up your empathy levels.

PART III

Montreal

ELI

The day my father received his diagnosis he changed genres. In the evening, when he telephoned to tell me the news, he claimed to have laughed out loud in the doctor's office.

"Can you believe it – a man who loves words, who loves the way they look but even more how they sound, who loves to roll them around in his mouth like a fine cigar – inoperable throat cancer. Isn't it fucking ridiculous?"

Yes, Dad, it is. Ridiculous. Ironic. A verse in an Alanis Morissette song. My father knew I wanted to ask the question but wouldn't, so he spared me. "Apparently I've got six months. Less time than it takes a baby to grow. Not a lot of time. Well boyo, that's the way the cookie crumbles. I've got to go now. Your mom's quite upset. I'll continue to do my part for now, but you'll need to take good care of her when I'm gone." When I got off the phone I cried. I was so angry. Angry at my father for sounding so cheery.

At first I thought he was going to write one last award-winning, gut-wrenching, lyrical book of poems: straight-ahead love poems, sublime profane sonnets dedicated to my mother. It would be his final lover's quarrel with life and death, and he would go out in one last poetic blaze of glory. But he had other ideas. One week later I opened up *The Mail and Post* to read a note from the editor-in-chief "Although all of us at the *Mail* are deeply saddened, as all Canadians will be, by the news that Adam Tredman shares with us in the pages of *The Mail and Post* today, we are heartened that he has decided to make his first foray into journalism with Canada's national newspaper, and that he will share his story with us in an exclusive column that will run every Monday on page D1." Aha, I got it. The Life section. It appeared my father and the editor at the *Mail* shared the same strain of humour.

I found the Life section, saw the smiling headshot of my father, and began to read. "On Deadline: a weekly column about living with dying."

Good morning. Or afternoon, as the case may be. My name is Adam Tredman and I'm dying. I'm also a recovering poet, or to be completely truthful, a poet who has never recovered, nor ever wanted to. This is the first piece of journalism I have ever written.

When I first heard the news from my doctor that I had six months to live, my thoughts turned to how I might respond to this news in poetry. I thought of Keats and of anyone else who had ever sat in a doctor's office and received the news. We all know we are going to die in the end, but we are all surprised in our own little ways when we get the news with a timeline attached.

Later that night, as I spoke with my wife about how our lives had changed, I realized that I would not write poems but would turn to that most immediate and, dare I say it in the pages of this newspaper, most ephemeral of literary arts – journalism – to report on my journey. Journalism is really the poetry of the day. It's all about how to say as much as you can in as little space as you can. Each week I will write a column about living with a death sentence. But do not despair, dear reader. Each week, this column will be a celebration of life, and, of course, dying.

My father's illness had turned his old hierarchy of writers – with journalists at the bottom and poets at the top – on its head.

His column went on like this for another seven hundred words.

"Hey Eli, your old man sends a sweet tweet," was how the Clerk of the Privy Council Office greeted me one Monday morning in the Langevin Block after a weekend I'd spent completely devoted to ensuring the well-being of Sophie and the kids. I'd turned off my BlackBerry, hadn't read the papers, hadn't thought about work while I was entertaining my children or sipping tea with Sophie. In the course of my conversation with the Clerk I learned that my father had 25,000 followers on Twitter. While a far cry from Ashton Kutcher's million or so best friends, my seventy-two-year-old father was apparently a minor celebrity in the Twitterverse. I signed up to follow him and over the ensuing week received updates like the following:

> Started to feel the pain today. Of course you know it's coming, but it really drives home the reality of your situation. Hard to describe.

And then, two hours later:

> Let me try. It's like the first shot in a long purposeless war fired on a deserted border where you're on the side you know will lose.

And three hours after that:

> Went to get a smoked meat sandwich at the Snowdon Deli. Not sure how long I'll be able to eat solid food. Got to enjoy every last bite.

And the following morning:

Couldn't sleep last night. Thought about tweeting but read Shakespeare instead. Lear. My all-time favourite play. Fuck, that Willy's good.

The sly bastard. Working in off-colour *double entendres*.

One afternoon, when the pain had just started, the coughing was sporadic, and he could still talk, I asked him whether he was writing any poetry. He shook his head. "Nah."

I asked him why. He shook his head again. "You wouldn't believe me if I told you."

"Try me."

"The stuff I'm going through is too serious for poetry." He held up his hand. "I know, I know. I know what you're going to say, but it's still true. If you talk to a young poet nowadays, it's all about the sound that consonants and vowels make when they're smashed up together, sort of like a verbal mosh pit or that crazy sampling stuff. But for me, poetry will always be about love, and death, and trying to capture it in time, in your own time, with your own words. But not my own death. Death in general.

"Remember that thought experiment, about how if you put a team of monkeys in a room and gave them typewriters, they'd eventually write the complete works of Shakespeare? It's true. They would. But the problem is it would take them fifty million years. I've often thought that if only I could live to be a thousand years, maybe just seven hundred and fifty even, I could write one play as good as Shakespeare's. But we run out of time. Being great is not just a function of talent in a vacuum. It's about how quick you can develop. You'll never read this in my tweets, or even in my column, but death is fucking depressing. That's one thing I promised myself when I started off. I wasn't going to be one of those poets whose books are a waste of a tree. I wasn't going to write like I was on Prozac. God, that shit makes me ill. Poetry should be fun. Death is not fun, despite what I say in my column or tweets."

His last column had been a satirical rant along the theme of: if you can't beat 'em you might as well join 'em. "You know, Eli, if I were starting all over again I'd become a journalist. They're the true poets. They have to say as much as they can in a few column inches. And more people read in the newspaper about where Brad Pitt took his brood of children than read anybody's poems. Journalism is where it's at. And sports or celebrity journalism is best. Didn't García Márquez once say that the first thing he read in the morning were the sports pages, because that's where you learned about how man handled his triumph and his defeat? I've always been envious of sports writers. Some of the best journalism is in the sports pages. Who was that guy, he used to write for the local paper, he was always about a hundred years old, always skated a little close to the homoerotic side, the way he described all those athletes? He was like a fucking Homer, the way he had these heroic adjectives he'd use over and over to describe how people would skate down the ice, or shoot, or swear, even when they were screwing up and weren't being good or brave? In his way, he was a poet."

I must have been looking at him strangely, because my dad just stopped. "You think I'm funny? You think your old man is talking too much? I've got to talk while I can, boyo. My fucking doctors want to cut out my tongue. It won't cure me but might give me another three months. What do you think of that? All those poems, and I end up having to decide whether I want to live a few more months without a tongue." And he laughed. Loudly.

Years earlier, when I was a boy, I'd always been amazed that my father seemed to have two laughs. One, his real laugh, where he'd sit and laugh and bob up and down, his face a mass of lines, his eyes narrowed to slits, like a glorious, peaceful Buddha laughing at some great cosmic joke. But he also had a second laugh, which was louder, and sounded a bit forced. I'd once asked him about his second laugh. He'd bounced me on his knee, put down *Treasure Island* or whatever book he'd been reading to me, and said, "Sometimes you have something to laugh about. So you laugh. Other times you feel like crying. So you laugh. Get it?"

It was on one of our walks together at Mount Royal that my father broke the news. "I've decided to go ahead with it."

We were up at the lookout, the city a giant's grey Lego set below. My father was leaning over the balustrade, looking away from me. When I was a boy he'd walked up the thousand steps with me and then bought me an ice cream as a reward for letting him carry me. "With the surgery?"

"Yes." My father turned around and looked into my eyes, daring me to challenge what was coming. "I wasn't planning to, but I'm doing it for your mother. She says she's not ready to be left alone." My father started walking away from the edge. "Do you know that I never once cheated on your mother?" He was walking fast now, not looking at me, almost talking to himself.

No Dad.

"True story. Not once. Never even thought about it. That might seem like small potatoes to your straitlaced generation, but in mine, and as a wild and crazy poet, that's about as good as it gets, like winning the fucking Nobel Prize. Very, very rare."

We walked in silence for a few minutes. The path was full of people talking and laughing, walking and running and biking. None of them looked like they were dying. "You know, I always thought that Naomi and I lived the life that Romeo and Juliet would have lived if only they'd had reasonable parents."

And I finally understood the poem my father had written when he was forty-eight about a middle-aged Romeo and Juliet. The friar hadn't been delayed and had gotten the message to Romeo in time. Romeo hadn't stabbed himself, Juliet hadn't taken the poison, and they'd had ten children and grown old and wrinkly and argumentative together, getting on each other's nerves by telling the same old boring stories over and over, in a handsome whitewashed villa in Verona.

One morning between meetings I sneaked away from the office to Sal's. I had it on my calendar as a personal appointment, but my assistant, Denise, knew where I was going. It was closing in on 11.30 a.m., and years of going to Sal's every five weeks or so had taught me it was the best time to get a haircut. Sure enough, he was finishing off some guy with short white hair who looked like an old centurion, and he was with me in five minutes. Sal was an old-school barber. Of course he was Italian. He still combed his silver-grey hair straight back and slicked it down with some grease or other. He always wore dark pants and a white shirt, wide open at the collar, showing off his grey curling chest hairs, like shark's teeth. He had the physique of a former natural athlete or strongman, still heavy and muscular with a respectable layer of fat that gave the impression it could be melted away in two weeks if only Sal wanted to. You sensed he still had the discipline.

Sal was fifty-four, and Sal's shop looked like it hadn't changed in fifty years. Black and white tile flooring – chessboard pattern – high leather seats, small mirrors. No surrenders to time, to whatever was the latest thing in hair salons. Old fashioned lighting. It was super clean. Naturally Sal's clientele were almost entirely men, although he did offer women's haircuts. Sal was a legend in Ottawa, his place tucked away downtown on Queen Street, just blocks away from Parliament Hill. Sal had been a proud Canadian for thirty-five years, emigrating from Sicily at the age of nineteen.

The mythology around Sal was that he had to flee Italy under cover of night when he eloped with a girl in the village who had been "promised" to the son of the local Mafia boss. Sal, ever the gentleman and never the boaster, had never quite refuted the story. Whenever anyone brought it up, Sal would nod and mutter a few words, and from the look in his eyes it was clear he was reliving those extraordinarily blissful days and hours of transgression in Sicily, out in the field, or perhaps behind some Roman ruins, and then the hours and days of fear that were only conquered by flight, being smuggled out on an oil tanker bound for the Greek islands, and then making his way with his love to Canada and building a kingdom in Ottawa.

He was most proud of a photo of himself that he kept just below the mirror. It was of a thin boy of about sixteen holding a comb and scissors beside a man in a barber chair. The man was the fattest man I had ever seen, and he had a look in his eyes that said *I own the world*. Beside Sal were four other men, tall, smirking. Sal's smile was innocent, proud, a boy on his way to becoming a man, confident in the promise of his talent. I had never asked Sal but had always assumed the man in the chair was the Mafia boss whose predestined daughter-in-law Sal stole. It was a beautiful photo in the way that all old photos were beautiful, in the way that people took the time to pose, in their respect for the camera, their sense of not being completely comfortable or trusting of its power, and in the way they showed up the present, with our snapshots of our lives, our sense of not documenting occasions but moments.

But for all his past, Sal was also a legend in Ottawa because of what he knew. Sal was illiterate in the narrow sense that he had never read a book in his life, indeed he had never learned to even read or write, but he knew everything there was to know in Ottawa, both in the present and in the future. Sal was our Delphic Oracle, predicting the results of every election in the last thirty years within three seats. Every politician of any political stripe who was running in Ontario, every politician who led a party, every flack who fancied himself a strategist, made the obligatory regular pilgrimage to Sal to consult him on his political future.

And Sal, bless his soul, was less complex than some of the oracles of old. He spoke plainly, not in riddles, and there was never any double or dramatic irony. And Sal's information and advice was especially valued by everyone who sat in his chair and entrusted themselves to his scissor and razor – and to his classic sense of masculine style – because Sal played no favourites, took no sides, played no games, spilled no secrets. Sal never betrayed a confidence, never failed a friend, never said a bad word about anyone, never gave away any state secret, never knowingly influenced the outcome of a battle the following day. And because of this, Sal was able to hear almost everything there was to hear in Ottawa, synthesize it, and pronounce judgment on the political fates. And, perhaps most surprisingly of all – and this was a testament to the high esteem he was held in by everyone who spoke to him – Sal had been able to do this for thirty years without ever making it into the papers. The media didn't know about Sal, or if they did, they were keeping him to themselves.

That morning we started off slowly, as we always did. Sal motioned me over with a wave of his apron, scattering the hair of the previous occupant of his chair with a flourish, calling me over in slow motion like a matador to a bull, without words, just a flick of an arm. I sat down, made myself comfortable, closed my eyes. I had never been one to spend a lot of time looking in the mirror, and I wanted to relax. Every five weeks I looked forward to visiting Sal, for the conversation that would inevitably arise and for the feeling of being taken care of in a way that I didn't often take care of myself. This was as close as I got to any form of pampering or physical care. It was my rough-hewn version of a spa. We didn't speak at all for the first five minutes. I enjoyed the blend of silence, radio, and the noise from the street through the open door. Then we started speaking. I always started first, always with the same question.

It was like a catechism between us. "So Sal, what's new?"

He didn't answer for ten seconds or so, kept cutting my hair, looking serious, admiring his own skill. He muttered under his breath, and then he mumbled, like someone pretending to be Brando pretending to be Don Corleone, except that the effect in real life was not as foolish as it appears here in print. "The people – ," and then he paused like any great orator beginning to warm up the crowd, until he was sure he had my attention, until he was sure I was waiting desperately for him to continue, even though he had me prisoner in his chair and I wasn't going anywhere, and I had come to listen to him with all my attention. He spoke softly, so I had to make an effort to hear him, and by making that effort I was already committing to meet him halfway, already signalling that I wanted to hear what he had to say: "The people don't want us to go." Then he went back to my hair. The Oracle had spoken.

One week later, Allan made one of the decisions that I am sure will come to define his career. He kept us out of the latest foreign war: on terror, dictatorship, injustice, fear, the latest threat to our way of life and freedom. This was the war that all our allies were supporting, the war where Allan, and by his decision Canadians, would stand almost alone in opposing, in declining to take up arms, in refusing to send our youngest and most vulnerable to fight and die for our right to wake up every morning in peace, to eat our preferred brand of cereal, drive our cars, work at our jobs, and come home to our smiling spouses and children. Sal, from the perch of his barbershop, had correctly read the mood of thirty-three million Canadians, not to go to war, at least not to the particular war we were being called to in that particular year of our mandate. But in case you think Allan was the twenty-first century incarnation of Mackenzie King setting foreign policy over an Ouija board, and I his mother's medium, we also did our scientific homework to corroborate what we and Sal were already thinking. Polling, town hall meetings, focus groups, over and over again all week, to prove what Sal already knew.

When I visited my father in hospital after his surgery, he was still asleep. He was as peaceful as I'd ever seen him. My mother was there by his bedside holding his hand. I was amazed at how small my father looked, how frail. He'd always taken pride in his physique – in an old-fashioned, dignified way, not an underwear model way – and he'd exercised almost every day of his life. Now for the first time he looked old, and I felt that something had shifted between us. My mother had been there for five hours. I asked her if she wanted to take a walk.

"How can I leave him?"

"He'll be okay." I took her down to the restaurant and bought her a coffee. She was trying hard not to, but she cried anyway.

"It's okay, Mom."

"No, Eli it's not okay. I don't want him to die. He's too young. He's too full of life. He doesn't deserve to have pieces of him cut away. Last night he kissed me like he did when we first got married, for hours. He said he wanted to remember what it was like."

"He wants to do this, you know. He wants you to be happy."

My mother started laughing and crying at the same time. "For me? I told him he should enjoy his remaining months. He better not be doing it for me, the stubborn goat. That's where you get your stubbornness, you know." And then she was off again, laughing and crying.

"Well it doesn't really matter. We have to be strong for him."

"Eli, you're the son. You can be as strong as you want. I'll just be there for him, okay?"

I'd come to see him before the operation. He was holding something in his hand and staring at it. It looked like a large beige plastic wafer. I handed him the smoked meat sandwich I'd brought him, what he'd jokingly referred to as his last supper, and asked him what he was looking at.

He put it down on his lap and took off his reading glasses. Waving his glasses around like a stage prop, he began talking. "This, boyo, is going to do to all your paper-obsessed luddites what Gutenberg did to those sorry monks monkeying around with their beautiful pictures and calligraphy." I didn't rise to the bait but waited for him to go on.

"Lovers of paper are fucked." He switched from his glasses to brandishing the plastic thing. "Do you know how long it takes to publish a book of poems from start to finish? Twice as long as it takes to have a baby. You send your fucking manuscript away, mostly in the mail, and it takes six months to hear back from the publisher, another six months of editing, and then six months if you're lucky or famous, a year if you're not, to get your book on the shelves. Two years. That sort of sentence gets you into a federal prison. This, my boy, is a Kin-dle. It can hold three hundred books. That number will likely double in a week. It's been launched by Amazon, and I've been working out a deal to load all my books, all twenty of them, on one of these as a special promotional package. They gave me one as an author's gift fully loaded with my poetic dream team. Starting with the big Willy. I've been reading *Othello*. Look at the print – it's not your regular computer screen. If you didn't know any better you'd swear it was paper."

"Pretty cool, Dad."

"Pretty cool? I get you, you know. You're already scared shitless you won't be able to buy any books soon, aren't you. No need to act tough in front of your old man. You've never liked change. Not since you were a boy. If we bought a new breakfast cereal or made your scrambled eggs a different way you'd get all worked up. You never went to a sleepover at a friend's house because you couldn't take the thought of sleeping in anybody else's bed but your own."

"But Dad – "

"Don't 'but Dad' me. I know you think you're pretty cool, you have a big job, and I know you've learned to fake it, but you can't take the boy out of the man. If you want to freak yourself out, get yourself a Kindle."

Then he went back to his reading as if I wasn't there and as if he wasn't reading the last book he would ever read with a tongue in his head. He was reading this book on some wafer-thin computer screen that was the result of a lot of smart people trying to figure out how to recreate the experience of holding a real book in your hand and reading it.

On my first visit to my parents' home after my father's operation, my mother greeted me at the door. When I asked how he was doing, she pulled me inside and said, "See for yourself."

He was draped across the sofa in the living room, in shorts and a T-shirt, looking every bit the disheveled but happy frat student, not like a seventy-two year-old man with an expiry date. He motioned me over to sit down beside him and offered me a beer. The TV was on loud on one of those reality shows. While I watched, amazed, he pulled a BlackBerry out of thin air and began typing away madly with two thumbs. This from a man who had refused to touch a typewriter his whole life because he thought it was an artificial machine that got between him and his muse – "a mechanical condom," as he'd once christened it in a poem. His whole literary life he'd written longhand only in those black notebooks that didn't have a name until an Italian company named Moleskine invented one, and my mother, bless her hidden stenographer's soul, had taken time out from being a celebrated professor of twentieth-century literature and self-professed feminist to type her husband's manuscripts like a dumbstruck amanuensis. Within seconds he'd passed me the BlackBerry. I read the message:

I can't get enough of these reality shows. It's a first-hand window on the painful decline of the one-way, passive medium.

He grabbed my arm and waved his hand toward himself. I realized he wanted the BlackBerry back. I passed it back to him, and he began hammering away with his thumbs. Again, seconds later he handed it back to me, and took a slow, careful swig of his beer. I wondered how you drank without a tongue, and read:

TV is so old, so boring. It's pure one-way communication, something Goebbels would have been proud of. There's no room to co-create. This obsession with so-called ordinary people is the last spasm, the death rattle of the old medium. Mark my words – TV will be dead in ten years.

"Before newspapers?"

Emphatic downward nod of the head. Saying, "Give me the BlackBerry" with his hands.

Don't get me started on newspapers. I love them to death. I love their feel. Their smell. The way they leave black smudges on my fingers and on the walls. Their crumple and crunch. How they're confident in their charms and don't try to seduce you like TV. But they're dead.

He left me with the BlackBerry and forgot about it for a while, and we watched how Jon and Kate were coping – not very well – with their octuplets and the accompanying stresses, the infidelities, the screaming matches, the money they weren't used to, and we sat there for hours, like good friends who are comfortable with the silence between them, who don't feel compelled to ruin the experience of being close together with the interposition of mere words.

One afternoon in late May, a couple of weeks after my father's surgery, I drove the two hours to Montreal to visit him. He was in
the back garden, stretched out on a reclining lawn chair, reading
Beowulf. I stopped at the fence and watched him for a few minutes.
The sun was low in the sky, but still warm, and he looked like a
lizard sunning himself on a rock, his body working hard to absorb
the remaining warmth.

When I was a few feet away, I said hello, and he put down his
book, and smiled, the skin on his face pulling away from his mouth,
so that the lizard had magically transformed itself into a hungry
dog. He put down *Beowulf* and picked up the BlackBerry, which
never left his side, and began typing away with his thumbs:

> God I love the old English poets, so much pleasure in the
> language without our modern affectations, the natural
> rhythms as opposed to manufactured ones, the compound
> adjectives, the "word-hoard," the almost, but just almost,
> fascination with bravery, the untainted hero-worship of
> men who could tame dragons and their own toothy fears.

He handed over the device. I read it and nodded. Impatient, he
grabbed my arm, wanting the BlackBerry back. He typed a bit and
then handed it over:

> I'm reading a lot of old Norse poetry now, all those legends.

Arm signifying pass it back.

> Do you know what the secret of happiness is?

I shook my head. Passed it back.

It's being content about where you are in time. Being happy when you're young and have no money or power. Being happy when you're working fifteen hours a day to build your career. Being happy when your children are young and keeping you awake at night, and your wife has no time for you and feels like a milk cow. Being happy when your children have left you and you're all alone. Being happy when your body starts to betray you, and you can't do the things you used to do when you were young, or worse, don't want to. And finally, enjoying the final journey, as much as you can.

Passed it back. Fast play of thumbs.

Do you know what my favourite story in Norse poetry is?

Shook my head. I too had stopped speaking aloud.

It's when everybody is gathered late at night in the longhouse and they're drinking and eating and spilling mead and food all over themselves and swearing and laughing and telling stories, some of them true, about war and love and death, and paying their respect to the heroes who are no longer with them, and you can smell the cooked flesh, and the sweat, and everybody's smelly, and a bird flies through the opening in the wall high up at one end, and makes its way, not too fast, not too slow, through the crowded hall, and some people notice but most don't because they're too busy drinking and eating and living, and then the bird flies out into the night at the other end, and nobody knows where the bird has come from and nobody knows where the bird is going,

but for one eye blink, one moment in time, that bird is in
the midst of the shouting and the living, and then it is gone.

He'd worn himself out with that last message. He put out a hand
for the BlackBerry, took it back, and passed me Seamus Heaney's
translation of *Beowulf*. He pointed his finger to where he'd left off
and closed his eyes. And so I read to him for thirty minutes about
the hero who sails to a distant land and comforts a frightened king
and slays a monster. And who in the end, when he's old and perhaps
his reflexes are not as sharp, and the sword is a little heavy, can't
resist the desire to save another kingdom and slay the monster's son
and be a hero, and so lays down his life and ends up the subject of a
poem that over a thousand years later was providing some comfort
to my father on a late spring afternoon in Montreal.

Later on that same visit, after my father had fallen asleep, my mother and I were drinking in the living room. Scotch and soda for her,
tea for me. I never could out-drink my mother. I asked her what
their secret was, what had kept them together all those years. I was
curious what Naomi, who had earned her tenure on the basis of her
second book, *From Muse to Medusa: Reversing the Male Gaze in the
Poetry of Twentieth Century Women,* would have to say about living
with the great Adam Tredman. But she didn't seem to think the
question was a worthy one. She actually shook her head. "Come
on, Eli, you know the answer to that one." I hoped she wasn't going
to say "communication."

"Every women's magazine will tell you that the foundation
of a good marriage is open and honest communication. Full stop.
I have no idea what the men's magazines say, although I can guess."
Wrinkling of her nose. Sip of her Scotch. She saw the look on my
face. "But don't worry, that doesn't begin to tell the half of it." She
put her feet up on the embroidered ottoman from Tashkent that

had been an anniversary gift from my father. "The older I get, the more I think it all comes down to chemistry. Smell. Pheromones. Good sex. Without that you're just friends." She saw the look on my face. Another sip of Scotch. "Sorry you asked?"

I didn't reply. I was admiring her for not dyeing her hair. It was a soft silvery grey. It didn't make her look older.

"I do concede you also require the absence of bad behaviour. Adam has been easy as husbands go. And as a poet, he certainly gave me nothing bad to write about in any of my books." She laughed. "Do you know when we first met, I thought I would give him just a little bit of a hard time. He was so sure his choice of reading would impress, that I'd think we had so much in common because we were both supposedly reading *Lord Jim*. He was holding it so I couldn't miss the title and would think what an amazing coincidence, I've got to go out with this guy. It was so misplaced and so charming at the same time, that thoughtless male confidence and scheming. So I teased him about *Nostromo* versus *Lord Jim*. Courage versus cowardice. Real manly stuff. Did you know that Hemingway once said the only two subjects worth writing about were war and impotence? A bit self-limiting, if you ask me, but he covered both of them reasonably well in *The Sun Also Rises*. Still, it's no wonder he blew his head off."

We sipped in silence. I had another question.

"What do you think of Dad's poetry?"

"It's pretty good. But does it matter what we think?"

"Do you think it will still be read in a hundred years?"

"Or a thousand? Like *Beowulf*? Is that what you're wondering?

"I said a hundred. A thousand might be a little ambitious."

"I think he has a good chance at a hundred, if people are still reading poetry." She tried not to let her voice crack. "Thanks for being here as much as you are. He's enjoying the time you spend together."

MICHAEL

The day my latest book was launched, I had high hopes. I know the analogy's both cloyed and hackneyed (and probably hyper-offensive coming from a man who obviously can only imagine such things) but I felt like for nine months, which was almost exactly the time it had taken me to write the book, I'd been carrying a baby.

It had woken me in the middle of the night, made me want to throw up more than once, and overshadowed almost all my conscious and unconscious hours. When it was finally out in the world, after the typically slow and painful delivery through the convoluted birth canal of editing and publishing, I felt like the proudest mother in the neonatal ward after giving birth to a ruddy, bright-eyed, strong-lunged, bouncing baby boy. And like every proud parent, I'd spent months agonizing over choosing a name. I wanted something that would be original but not cute, that would mean something both to me and to others, and that would carry my boy reliably and proudly through his earliest years and all through his life. So I'd given the rectangular, paper child of my poor sweating brain an evocative name: *Strong and Free in the Twenty-First Century*.

My book was an assessment of the challenges confronting Canada on the cusp of the new millennium. These included globalization and the flight of capital, climate change, ethnic strife, the uncertainty around the oil sands during the accelerated start of a world energy transition and economic crisis. I threw in a smattering of region-al wars, the early warning signs of freshwater shortages, and the ever-reliable presence of disease (the rise of vaccine-resistant strains of flu and antibiotic-resistant infections). On the domestic front,

I highlighted regional political affiliations and balkanized parliaments, child poverty, the never-dead zombie virus of federal-provincial relations, budget deficits, and the increasing feeling on the part of many Canadians that parliamentary democracy and party politics were irrelevant to their lives. In the final chapters I offered my prescription for how Canada could return to and leverage its traditional strengths of multiculturalism, pluralism, geography, proximity to the US, the British parliamentary tradition, fairness in health care and education, and a steady outlook that was sitting prettily between free-market individualism in the US and the safety of the destiny of the collective in Europe. I argued these structural advantages would allow Canada to chart a new course and retake our position as a global leader in the new century and millennium.

It was a big book, if I must say so myself, in all senses of the word. It had big ideas, strong writing, timeliness, and relevance. It was a clear contender for all of Canada's public policy writing prizes. I was set to give a reading at the launch party at the Royal York, and I'd given an interview scheduled to run on the front page of *The Mail and Post*. Everything was going according to plan when fate and the modern world conspired to fuck everything up. The day before the launch, an American entertainer by the name of Michael Jackson had the temerity to die, possibly of a heart attack, possibly of criminal negligence, at his home in Bel-Air while preparing for his latest global comeback tour.

And, faster than Michael could moonwalk through your living room, my interview was whisked off the front page, exiled to one of those sub-sections on the inside of the front section where the national and international news rent space. The world stopped turning on its axis for a few days as typically serious scribes outdid each other in their zeal to read sense and meaning into the story of a man-child who apparently had been subjected to some kind of talent abuse by his father as a boy, who grew up singing and dancing

when everybody around him was crawling, who could entertain
the bobby socks off the most cynical teenyboppers and their parents. Who, in the words of one colleague, represented the boomers'
safe offering to their children of a sanitized rebellion they could live
with, that was a pale – no pun intended – shadow of their own former youth of sex and drugs and rock and roll. And whose whiter
and whiter shades of personal pale were the symptom of either
some exotic disease or a prolonged, very public attempt by a man to
obliterate his former self, a Hollywood version of Jane Urquhart's
The Underpainter. (Thank God I didn't read any public comment from
her.) You might have been forgiven, if you'd just landed by space-
ship on this planet, for thinking that Michael J was an artistic Jesus
Christ, sent down by his father to save us from our sins and bring absolution in his footsteps and smooth moves. And we were not really
all zombies marching behind him in what would no doubt be apparent to historians looking back on these years from the safe vantage
point of time as the final call-out of our culture and civilization.

I hadn't seen our society in such a total state of mourning since
the death of Diana, dubbed "The People's Princess" by Blair's communications guy, when complete strangers – and I use that word
like a poet here, like a sleek missile on its way to its destination
with all its meanings nestling in its payload – bawled on prime-
time TV and placed flowers at makeshift memorials fit for a child
saint. [That communications guy is of course Alastair Campbell,
the British journalist and author who served as Prime Minister
Tony Blair's Director of Communications and Strategy from 1997
to 2003. Campbell resigned during an investigation into the death
of British biological warfare expert David Kelly following intense
questioning before a House of Commons committee.] Everyone
blubbered to any journalist willing to listen about how much
Michael J and his music had meant to them, and how they were
going to go out and buy his collected oeuvre for their children so

they, too, could have that experience. All of Michael's weirdness – his outfits, his wigs, his pajama outings to court, his mishaps on the set of Pepsi commercials, his sleepovers, his dangling his son out of a window, his strange, brief, temporary marriages, his child molestation charges, and the multi-million dollar settlements with those children's parents – all of this was overlooked, or forgiven, or simply swept away in the tsunami of manufactured grief.

I shouldn't have been so shocked. Five years before, *The Mail and Post* had won a newspaper war, and in one of war's easiest ironies we'd become our own enemy. Like a sleepy nation before a war, we'd been sanctimonious and dull. We didn't choose to enter the quarrel with a younger, upstart rival eager to expand, confident it could bring us to our knees with money and an army of writers ready to impale us with their bayonets of wit, but we followed Polonius's timeless bar fight advice: avoid a fight, but once in, make sure you win. In our case, we hired mercenaries, battle-hardened from foreign wars, to teach us pasty pacifists how to brawl.

My editors got younger, and we went, after over a hundred years of tradition, to full-colour design from black and white. We moved over and made room for more sports and entertainment and lifestyle articles. We hired stylish, young, attractive columnists who littered their prose with gentle profanities and could wax eloquent about both Kierkegaard and Brazilian waxing. We chronicled the romps and escapades of celebrities as proficiently as anyone else on the planet. At the end of it, when we won, I felt relieved and old-fashioned, like a Second World War general surviving into the 1960s. In the new world, celebrities were our immediate family of gods, materialism and entertainment our new religion. Like the Romans, we'd swapped out our moral calendar and sense of time, so we confused what was happening today with what would be important tomorrow.

My book still went on to be a bestseller by our modest Canadian standards, and was picked up by a few intellectuals and political types in Europe, but it never gained the popularity of my book about Laffrey or had the impact it might have had if it had been launched as planned.

[As I pause to look back at the preceding paragraphs, it's clear I've left too much bitterness behind in the words, too much unfiltered emotion. It's not very attractive, now that I reread it, not at all how I want to be known. I'll have to make sure I talk to my editor about cleaning this section up. I still think my thesis is good, something about our modern preoccupation with celebrity, the reduction of our ability to think about complicated things, the decline of our culture, but someone less conflicted and with colder eyes will need to airbrush my thinking, apply Botox, and make it clean and presentable for its close-up.]

My memory of my book's stillborn entry into the world is even more acute because I saw Eli later that week. He was coming into a Starbucks on Yonge Street while I was heading out. He'd been at the top of his game for about a decade, and he looked it. Trim, still young, greying around the temples, carrying himself well, no wasted movement. As always, he was friendly. We chatted briefly, like the professional acquaintances we had been for over twenty years.

"You're keeping Allan on a short leash these days. He's not losing his touch, is he?" I teased him about not letting the PM do very many interviews in recent days, and Eli laughed, said something polite and self-deprecating without giving anything away. I wanted to tell him that I understood, that I even sympathized, but I felt that would be too much like fraternizing with the enemy. I wanted to tell him I understood his job was like being an artist where you put your soul and mind into creating a painting before handing it over to someone. And then that person has all night to paint over it, adding colour here, a brushstroke there, downplaying certain elements, changing the composition, and then exhibiting it for the world to see. I wanted to tell him that I thought he was very good at what he did, but I didn't. Instead, we made small talk, about the weather, politics, and hockey, the holy trinity of Canadian males' conversations. As I walked away into the crowded streets, I found myself wishing I'd asked him to sit down, and we could have talked, not about politics or work, but as old friends.

ELI

Sophie had been dropping hints for eighteen months, ever since she became pregnant with our fourth child. The hints became pretty unsubtle pretty quickly. She had been saying it like it was a foregone conclusion or a fait accompli. I hated it when she said the word. It sounded obscene to me, criminal, insane like the story in the newspaper about the man in Germany whose fantasy was to be eaten by another human being, so he put an ad on the Internet and found a self-professed cannibal. The two met over the Internet and agreed to meet at the cannibal's apartment. The man with the fantasy took a bath, and presumably some serious painkillers, the cannibal cut off his penis, and started to eat it. In the end the guy died. Everybody at work was talking about having it done, without reticence, like a trip to the dentist or the garage. Almost every guy my age I worked with had had one, and they made jokes about it even when women were around. It was offered as a ready explanation for why Henry couldn't make a meeting or why Bob was taking Friday off, but I must have been old-fashioned or particularly squeamish, because I couldn't bear to tell my father. He would have thought I was castrating myself. I couldn't help thinking about palace eunuchs or unlucky young boys without balls but with beautiful voices singing their broken little hearts out in choirs in the Middle Ages for the pleasure of big fat bishops. At the very least it sounded to me like a sexual lobotomy.

At first I laughed it off with Sophie. She got offended. I hoped she was joking, but gradually, after weeks of discussions that turned into fights, I realized she was serious. For months it was all I obsessed about when I went to bed and when I woke. Finally, early in 2009, I saw my family physician to get a referral. He was very jovial about it, but I started feeling dizzy when he referred to it as sterilization. I thought about Nazi Germany and "mental defectives." He told me I needed to be sure about it because you wouldn't believe how many twenty-two-year olds he saw in the office who wanted a sure form of birth control and who thought that when they'd finally found that special someone they could come back and get it all reversed. He went to great pains to tell me that while it could be physically reversed, in the sense of sewing the vas deferens tubes back together, it rarely worked because sperm are very sensitive and they get damaged when they shoot across the seams through the welded fleshy pipe.

For some reason, I always thought they opened up your abdomen while you were sitting down in a comfortable chair, perhaps with a curtain falling over your chest. When I met the urologist for my consultation, he handed me a crudely drawn pamphlet that looked like a drawing on a bathroom stall wall, and after looking at it, I understood for the first time they went in through your scrotum, right between your testicles. I tried to avoid hyperventilating. He usually did these on a Friday. You took the day off and then you had the weekend to recuperate. He told me I needed to shave the front of my scrotum the day before, and I should wear tight underwear because they'd use them to stop the bleeding.

He would freeze me with the tiniest needle, then make a very small hole. Just like this, as he held his thumb and index finger half a centimetre apart. He would pull out one of the vas deferens tubes, cut it and loop it around on itself. He would use the same hole to do the other side, then he would put in just one stitch, and I would be good to go. I should have my wife drive me to the hospital, and I should bring an ice pack to put on my lap. Then I should go home and take it easy. Watch TV. Take advantage of my wife's pity.

Have her bring me beer, while I sat and relaxed. Make sure the kids didn't jump on me because it would really, really hurt and I would scream at them. Don't be a hero. No contact sports for a week.

It's the surest form of birth control, safer then the pill, more reliable than condoms. I asked if it's true the tubes sometimes re-attach of their own accord. He told me he'd never heard of it, but winked at me and said, "But I can't do anything about the milkman." Wise guy. Sex will look the same and feel the same. Most of what comes out isn't sperm, it's the propellant for the sperm. When I walked out of his office, the receptionist gave me a date six weeks out. I was too embarrassed to ask if they ever cut the wrong tube, or cut a nerve by accident. I'd read too many articles about prostate cancer. I wasn't too keen on impotence or incontinence.

When it was one week away, I called up to reschedule, claimed I had to travel for work. I made another appointment for two months out, in April. Sophie made it clear I could choose between having a vasectomy or never having sex again. I felt like a bull with a ring through his nose, being led passively to the slaughter. More like a bull with a ring through his scrotum.

I couldn't sleep the night before. I didn't talk much that morning as Sophie drove. She offered to come up with me, but I told her to wait downstairs. I wanted to be alone. The waiting room was crowded, and I worried that everyone knew why I was there. I tried to appear nonchalant, as if I were just waiting for a check-up, intently read the magazines without remembering anything about the latest war or music or movie, sat the way I imagined I would sit if I were relaxed. When the orderly called my name, I got up and walked cheerfully over. As we turned the corner and were out of sight of the rest of the waiting patients, he asked me how I felt about this. I smiled.

"As good as you can, I guess, eh?" he offered with a gentle grin, as if to say, *You poor sucker, I'm so glad I'm not you, I'm so glad today that I don't have a wife who I've impregnated multiple times, who loves me but doesn't love condoms, and who is making me go through with this so we can have sex without thinking or worrying, like we did when we were young.*

I smiled back noncommittally. He led me to a room where there was another orderly. This one looked like Salvador Dalí, with slicked-back hair and a dashing moustache. He had a glint in his eye and spoke slowly as he padded around the room readying instruments and cloths. "Lie down here and pull your pants down. Don't worry, you won't feel a thing. I had it done twenty years ago after my fifth child. Best thing I ever did."

He prepared the tray for the surgeon. I looked away. He made the obligatory joke to put me at ease: "We just found out the doctor's sick today. He asked me to do it." And it worked. I laughed. When the urologist entered the room, he was jovial too. We were just three men taking it easy and shooting the breeze. We could have been at a bar or fishing, except that one of us was lying on his back with his underwear down and his shaven balls exposed.

As the surgeon was dabbing red-coloured disinfectant that looked and seemed to smell a bit like dried blood on my inner thighs, Salvador leaned over, touched my arm conspiratorially, and said, "You know, it's the strangest thing, but you're going to want it even more afterwards. You know, if today you like it three times a week, after it's done you're going to want it three times *a day*. I don't know why. Must be psychological. There's no medical reason why it should be so. Must be a guy thing." I chuckled heartily because it seemed like the right response. Maybe it was true.

The surgeon gently moved my penis to the side. Then the first needle. It pricked, like a malevolent mosquito bite. Then another one, and I didn't feel a thing this time. I only knew the doctor was cutting open my scrotum from the tugging. It was as if someone had attached a piece of string to my balls and was yanking away.

The first vas deferens was cut and looped while we talked about my job and the news. Talking had always helped me to relax. When he did the second one I felt a sickening pain and yelped. My leg jerked. The surgeon pulled away, looked surprised and offended. I was lucky he didn't accidentally cut my penis off. It was like he'd taken my left testicle in his hand and squeezed. I worried he'd made a mistake, but it was okay. Then it was the sewing, that strange sensation of feeling the needle going in and out, and my scrotum pulling, but without pain.

When it was done, I walked gingerly out of the day surgery clinic, hoping everybody assumed I was just a relaxed, slow-moving guy, and not a man who had just had his tubes tied. Sophie was waiting in the van with the bag of frozen peas. Like most women, and unlike most men, she actually read instructions, read the brochure I'd been given, told me we could resume "sexual relations" when it felt comfortable, usually in a week. And in the space of part of a morning, I had joined the ranks of what our country's highest ranking Cabinet minister jocularly referred to as the "medically altered." I got a plain brown paper bag to take with me. Inside it were some more instructions and two small plastic bottles. In twelve weeks and sixteen weeks I was supposed to come in the bottles and bring them to the hospital within two hours of creating the samples. I buried the bag under my clothes in the bottom drawer of my dresser.

The lab only took samples one day of the week, and twelve weeks later I was scheduled to take an early flight with Allan to New York. So I set the alarm, and as gently as possible woke Sophie up. She helped me accomplish the task, I left for the airport, and then she rushed down to the hospital lab when it opened, with our four children in tow, to drop off the plastic container in the plain brown paper bag.

Someone once asked British Prime Minister Harold Macmillan

what he considered to be the greatest challenge for a politician. Without missing a beat, Macmillan replied, "Events, dear boy, events." We hadn't chosen to be heading into an election for a second term as the global markets melted down in a Chernobyl of financial pseudo-science, but there we were. We realized how bad things had become when we were in New York in July. Allan had been scheduled to give a speech on Wall Street for four months. At the previous week's Cabinet meeting, we had debated strategy. Half the Cabinet had wanted to come out strongly and pitch a package of economic stimulus and support. The other half had argued for Allan to keep a steady hand and not spook the markets. Talk the situation down. Avoid creating a self-fulfilling prophecy by acknowledging the direness of the situation. We had been deadlocked, and Allan had said he would think about it. But that day in New York, after the cab ride from the airport, Allan had made up his mind.

Prime ministers don't normally take cabs. It violates the most rudimentary conception of security and drives the RCMP nuts, but on occasion Allan insisted. It was part of his image and character and way of working, and the Mounties let him have his way as long as they were confident the cabbie in question had no idea who he was driving, and as long as Allan agreed that a member of his security detail ride with him. For those of you who don't know this, a cab ride is, for every dollar spent, by far and away the best way to research public opinion in any city in the world. After a haircut with Sal, of course. Cabbies know everything. Just spend forty bucks, take a cab, and you will learn in half an hour what it will take a public opinion research firm tens of thousands of dollars and days, if not weeks, to articulate in a fancy report, complete with graphs and PowerPoint speak.

The cab driver had beside him on the passenger's seat *The Wall Street Journal* and *The New York Times*, which was in the throes of a death watch, lurching from week to week with new stories about creditors that had begun nervously circling, somewhat embarrassed about holding the life jacket for a media institution, but circling nonetheless. Allan, perhaps searching for the opening anecdote for the speech he was to give in less than an hour, asked the cab driver what was new.

"What's new," the cabbie began rhetorically, in an Eastern European accent. "What's new is that nothing is new. It's the same old game it's always been throughout the long bloody death march of history. The rich screw the poor. The police spend their time putting the poor people in jail, but the real bandits are the ones in suits who sit in those fancy offices and dream up fancy ways to screw the average person, like you and me. They're the true criminals, the scum of the earth." He was exaggerating every syllable, and with his accent and intonation he sounded like the Count from Sesame Street. He turned a corner philosophically.

"But the real tragedy is that nothing will happen to them, to these scum. In fact they are getting money, these bailouts, to spend more money. They are being rewarded for their incompetence. They get to go home and play with their children and drink in their fancy kitchens and play in their fancy pools, and screw their expensive wives. This is a crazy country, you know, that's horny for its capitalists the way it is horny for its entertainers, that rewards them with money, even when they lose billions, our billions. In my country, which is Romania, a beautiful country, the most beautiful country in the world, they'd know what to do with these bandits, these criminals. Oh yes. They'd march them out of their fancy offices and round them up in a public space and you know what they'd do?" He looked in the rear-view mirror. It was clearly a rhetorical question.

"They'd cut their dicks off. That's what should happen to every one of these fancy Wall Street bankers. What do you think, huh?" and he looked again at us in the rear-view mirror, his eyebrows raised. "Line them up against the wall, pull down their fancy pinstriped pants and their monogrammed boxer shorts, make them hold out their dicks in their hands, and then cut them off." He took his right hand off the steering wheel and made a downward chopping motion. "Whoosh. Like this. That would solve a lot of problems. How many bankers would take your money again if they had the memory of having their dicks cut off? You could make the Harvard MBA graduating class watch. It would really be a great ethics lesson. Maybe, if those fancy bankers lost their dicks, they wouldn't even have the same urge any more to cheat and steal. What do you think?"

He was silent for a while, pleased perhaps with the image he had created for us of a group of dickless investment bankers realizing the error of their ways. "So," he said, partially changing the topic, "what do you two fine gentlemen do? Are you in finance perhaps?" I noticed a grin in the rear-view mirror.

"No, no," Allan said. "Far from it. We're in an *honourable* profession. We're politicians."

"Ah, *politicians*," our driver said, licking his lips, as he drew out the word, making it sound like "morticians." "The bankers' tricks are making politicians look good. So, if you don't mind me asking, are you politicians going to save us from the evil bankers? Are you going to follow the advice of my country and cut off a few dicks?"

Allan laughed. He was pleased. "You never know."

Allan had his anecdote and had made his decision. In his speech at noon, ostensibly being delivered to Wall Street but really to the voters back home from the height of the international podium, he acknowledged the real hardship that both Americans and Canadians were facing, and he promised to throw the full weight of his government behind ensuring that the average Canadian was not left out alone in the capitalist cold.

That afternoon in New York we had a gap of about an hour between meetings. Allan was tired of sitting in boardrooms high up in the sky, and he wanted to go for a walk around Manhattan. The security men hated these incognito walkabouts, but Allan had no time for worries. Like many politicians, he craved the proximity of crowds and had an inborn distrust of solitude. He loosened his tie and threw his jacket over his shoulder before we were out the door. His security detail split in two – two men in front, two behind – but if anybody in New York City wanted to do harm to the Prime Minister of Canada, his unsmiling RCMP guard would not be able to do anything, for pedestrians were everywhere. It was only mid-afternoon, but in many places we could only see the sun reflected in the steel and glass buildings that were like canyon walls. The crowd was flowing around us like a flesh and blood river, and I felt like a salmon swimming upstream.

The skyscrapers were bright, like the models in a fashion magazine. But every few blocks we passed a stone church, squatting and serene in the shadows of the taller buildings, like a plainer sister among her supermodel siblings. The stone churches were dark and stolid in their reluctance to reflect the passage of time, the ebb and flow empire. Despite the economic crisis, the glass towers were still full enough with men shouting into phones and trading their de-rivatives.

Allan was talking loudly and laughing and watching everyone rushing around him in a hurry to get somewhere. Everyone was talking madly on cell phones and BlackBerrys, clutching briefcases and purses and shopping bags, and Allan and I were feeling like students again, with no responsibilities of our own and time on our side. We heard a rhythmic pounding coming from up ahead but assumed it was construction and thought nothing of it. When we were close enough, we saw a man hunched over and sitting on a plastic pail in the middle of the wide sidewalk. He was hammering out a drumbeat with wooden blocks on tin buckets. His hands were a blur. He had eyes only for the surfaces he was bringing together. Allan and I stopped to watch and listen, and the buildings, the crowds, and the sleek cars flying by like the personal spaceships in a science fiction movie disappeared. In the middle of Manhattan we could hear nothing but the sound of wood on tin. Soon a crowd gathered, pulled from the stream. Like fish they were gasping for air. The man kept drumming, head down, oblivious to the pleasure he was creating and to the coins falling like raindrops at his feet. Allan pulled out a handful of American dollar bills and placed them with the solemnity of an offering in front of the drummer. We stood there listening until it was time to go back inside for our next meeting, and we could delay no longer.

The night before this story began, Sophie and I were lying in bed talking before making love. Like many husbands and wives closing in on middle age, I imagined, we were talking about the kids, how funny they were, how good, how smart, how kind. We congratulated each other on being so fortunate. We wondered silently and separately what we had done to deserve such luck. She was telling me about the crazy things our two middle children had said that day when I was at work. Ben, who was five, had told her that when I died he was going to marry her. Hannah, our only daughter, the eight-year-old child who had no fear of anything except large dogs, who loved motion and speed in all its real and imagined forms, had declared that when she grew up she would buy herself a plane and fly it, and fly it fast. And our oldest, Noah, the one who was born blue, had recently entered adolescence with a perfect complement of brain cells and without a mixed-up bone in his body.

Zach, the baby, was keeping Sophie up a lot at night, and she was tired all the time. She was telling me how she felt old, how when she looked in the mirror she saw wrinkles around her eyes, how they were even deeper when she smiled. "That's an easy one," I joked. "Don't look in the mirror or smile ever again."

She playfully punched me in the shoulder, accused me of not listening. When I leaned over to kiss her, she gently pushed me away, determined to make me listen some more. "I feel so old," she told me again. "Look at my roots: I have so many grey hairs." She wondered if she should cut her hair, if it would make her look or feel younger.

I wanted to tell her that she was beautiful, that she was young, but she would have thought I was biased or stupid or flattering her or just trying to get her into bed, even though I had already done that. She was only forty-two and I was forty-four. She could have passed for twenty-five. We would have been senior citizens or likely already dead if we'd been born a hundred thousand years ago. We'd have spent most of the twenty-five years or so of our lives living in a cave. Instead of flying around Canada and to other countries on government planes, I'd have been out hunting woolly mammoths, and she would have been home tending the fire and nursing babies. She would probably look a lot older and hairier.

That night, in hyper-modern 2009, we were only halfway done, still raising babies, entering our prime. I too was finally going grey without any help, and putting on weight around my waist. Some of the pants of my good suits were feeling tight. I found myself appreciating the pants with expensive and practical but still fashionable German waistbands that could stretch up to an inch. I was tired, too, from work and the constant flow of babies, and I got up sometimes in the middle of the night or early morning to pee, like my father whom I used to pity for that reason, but most of the time I felt as young as I did when I was a boy. Of course, I had the adrenalin rush of work to tire me out, the types of things that get boys excited, the feeling that you were taking a fort or saving the world, or rescuing your brothers-in-arms from certain death and defeat. Sophie, although she spent her time with children all hours of the day, was the one dealing with grown-up things.

I wanted to tell her that babies are only young for a short time – which she already knew – and that one day soon when the baby work was over, she would feel young again and she would have time spreading out in front of her without a wrinkle or a worry. Instead I stroked her dark hair, which I forgot she then dyed to cover up the traces of grey, and I reminded her of the time we were on vacation in Maine, with the three kids we had then.

We had spent the day playing on the beach, finding snails and crabs and setting them free, and letting the sun work its soothing cancerous magic on our bodies and our minds. In the evening we had gone to dinner at a popular family restaurant on the coast. Rustic tables and chairs. A blazing fire pit where they baked organic pizzas. Sophie had ordered a glass of wine and got carded. She was thirty-eight at the time and couldn't stop smiling all through dinner. Later that night when the kids were asleep, we had sneaked into the bathroom, closed the door, and made love like we used to when we were young and had all the time in the world.

Sophie finally let herself be persuaded by my bedtime anecdote and we stopped talking. Less than eight hours later, I would get a phone call from a former friend.

MICHAEL

You're probably wondering why I made the call to Eli that late September morning. Why didn't I just hang up and forget about what Allan had said after he thought the BlackBerry was off? You might assume it was because I thought what Allan had said about Canadians having to "put up or shut up" was too good a story to pass up and, to be honest, it was. But that wouldn't have come close to explaining things. Yes, the *story* is what all of us in journalism hunger for; it's what we love to uncover and to tell the world, before and better than anyone else. But each of us has great stories that we carry with us that never see the light of day – because we're saving them, or because telling them might have consequences that we couldn't live with, or because of a higher purpose that's served by not telling them, like the old standbys of national security or public safety or even, in some cases, love.

I never blamed my mother for anything she did, and I never blamed my father for anything he didn't do. But ever since I came home early from that chess tournament and found my mother with another man, I always felt there was nothing more important in life than the truth, and that the real test of integrity is when you say the same thing in the same way to everyone, use the same words in public as you do in private. When you decide to run for public office, and when the public puts their trust in you to serve them, I believe you're signing on to a higher standard of truth and authenticity, just like you accept a higher standard of courage when you join the Marines. And it's a burden you take on willingly, with full awareness and understanding. With a private comment that was

211

so obviously real and so at odds with his public words and public persona, I thought Allan was flunking the basic test in a big way. And Canadians had a right to know.

ELI

Our meeting that morning was quick. We had worked together too long and survived too many campaigns to need many words to communicate our thoughts to each other. We all knew Allan was nervous, that he realized he might have ended his chances for a second term with one stupid ten-second comment, but he had always been good at turning his emotions on and off at will, as if his face were a handsome TV screen that projected only when he desired. He was on his best behaviour when we gathered at 24 Sussex Drive to plan our strategy for the day. We sat in the living room, sprawled across the furniture like university students, not like serious, formal men who were beginning to go grey and who were running the country. I was in my element, for some reason that my genes or upbringing didn't adequately explain: calmest when things were darkest, able to dispense with all the other usually ever-present distractions and focus on the one or two things that matter in a crisis.

Ryan, my young, conscientious, and brilliant second-in-command, the one who had been there with Allan that morning and forgot to turn off his BlackBerry, greeted me outside. He looked like he had just run over a child. His body was trembling slightly, he was biting his lower lip, and he was holding back tears. He handed me his resignation letter, which I tore up and threw dramatically in the garbage. I gave him a hug, told him he was a good person who did a good job, that he was not going anywhere, and that I needed his help. He went to splash water on his face and forget what he'd done. When he came back he was ready to work.

As was Allan's custom, he let the rest of us do most of the

talking. He nodded every so often and occasionally asked a brief question, but we did the heavy lifting. I had always been impressed by Allan's willingness to let others help him, which is a much rarer quality than it sounds. Most people with a lot of vision and power assume they have to think through everything themselves and believe that everything has to turn out exactly the way they have envisaged it, often years before anyone else could begin to imagine it. It takes incredible discipline to trust others to do the right thing, to harness one of the most powerful human desires – to help and to have influence. In so doing, you perhaps settle for a little less than the perfection you have created in your mind, but you achieve, in the end, a better result.

Not surprisingly, we had two diametrically opposed alternatives: status quo, otherwise known as "ignore and carry on," or "acknowledge and apologize." Both had worked for politicians in the past. Someone asked if we could do focus groups. We could, but they would be too late to help us. We had only hours, perhaps minutes, to make up our minds about whether to act or not. No time for science and research. We had to rely on our instincts. Place bets without any scientific way to predict outcomes. Someone once said a decision is only a real decision if you don't have all the facts. And you never do. If you apologize unnecessarily, you run the risk of blowing up the incident, drawing people's attention to a minor thread in the tapestry of a campaign and ripping a large hole in it. If you wait too long, and you learn that an apology is necessary and is the only thing that will save you, you have waited too long and you are lost, for people will think your apology grudging, insincere, too little too late – and they will be right. The pundits who know about such things will not only criticize your lack of empathy and your integrity. They will take easy aim at your inability and that of your advisers to correctly read the public's mood. They will slam your lack of judgment and criticize you for reacting to events instead of shaping them. You will become a recurring footnote in the annals of political ineptitude.

We all agreed it was a screw-up; where we differed was in how to fix it. Don Melrose, our chief of staff, an old-school political ascetic from the Laffrey years, who early on in his career renounced the pleasures of the world and took a vow of chastity and obedience to the High Church of Politics, was married to the Party and to all those who served it faithfully. He spent even his sleeping time dreaming of political wars and winning. Don argued passionately and cogently and convincingly for riding it out, for not stooping to respond, for minimizing the gaffe. I listened respectfully, neither interjecting nor questioning, and then argued the opposite, for a quick, sincere, effective apology, for putting the Prime Minister's fate in the voters' hands, for dealing with this situation the way he had dealt with everything his entire career, not overthinking, not getting too complicated, not strategizing his way into a fiasco.

In the end, it wasn't much of a debate. Some leaders like to engage in a roundtable debate, like Kennedy or Clinton, to hear disparate views from around the room, and wait until the very last person has spoken and the last argument made before they make up their mind. Allan had always been different. Although he never wore a watch or paid any attention to time, Allan respected time: his own and that of those he worked with. And so he preferred to have his team think through an issue and then come to him with a unified recommendation. In less than thirty minutes we were done. It fell to me to synthesize the discussion and make the recommendation.

"We can't wait for the news story. Whoever tells his story first usually wins. Whoever tells his story first and best almost always wins. The person who tells his story first and best and who has the right people corroborating his story always wins. We need to issue an apology within the next forty-five minutes. We should put it on YouTube and send out a teaser on Twitter. If Ryan can get the video team ready, I will start writing. After we tape, I will make a couple of heads-up calls, and the right people will respond once the video is out there."

Because I was responsible for communications and I was the one making the recommendation, Allan accepted it without question or modification. It had almost always been this way, ever since he was first elected MP. Sometimes over the years he had asked a question, or expressed some discomfort with what I had recommended, but in the end he had always invested his trust, because that, too, was one of his strengths as a leader. He also made a joke that day, a variation of which he had always made when we were about to set forth to do battle or on a quest where there were many risks. The joke was always the same, delivered in a low-key way, with a smile, designed to help us both relax. "No worries, Eli, but if this backfires, and I lose the election, you're fired."

In the early years of the twentieth-first century, we had been treated to a parade of apologies. Politicians apologizing for lying, cheating flamboyantly on their wives, and taking bribes. Athletes apologizing for taking steroids and for refusing to come clean in front of child fans and grizzled congressional committees. Teary-eyed actors and rock stars apologizing for behaving badly on planes, in nightclubs and with the hired help, or punching out the paparazzi. And executives, in their stiff way, apologizing for insider trading and for neglecting to protect the integrity of their mission and the interests of their shareholders. After all this, the apology had become both an anthropological art form and a religious rite. In the PR profession, there were people who earned a comfortable living just crafting apologies for the rich and famous who had to beg for forgiveness.

Fifteen minutes later, I had written the short remarks. I reviewed the text with Allan. He read it over slowly, as if he had all the time in the world. He crossed out a few words with his

Montblanc pen and added a few others in his careful handwriting. Then he took twenty minutes to get comfortable with it.

Half an hour after we ended our meeting, we were in Allan's office, about to start taping. I had told him to take off his jacket and tie. His shirt was light blue, which looks good on TV and conveys more ordinariness than blinding, master-of-the-universe white. He did it in one take. As always, he had absorbed the spirit and some of the words of the speech and made them his own. It was the same but better.

MICHAEL

I watched the speech on YouTube. As I listened, I could see some-where in the imagined background Eli bent over his computer like a crab or a worshipper, choosing every word to convey his desired meaning and to fit Allan's cadence. And Allan, easily the most bril-liant orator this side of the 49th parallel, compared favourably with Obama by many – even me – delivered each word as if the world depended on it.

Studies show that when we watch someone speaking on TV, we focus most of our attention on how they look. Do they look trust-worthy? Are they nice? Would we invite them over for a barbecue? Would we approve of them dating our daughter? What do their clothes convey about them?

After we've taken in their appearance, we listen to what they say. In the overall impression that is created, a godforsaken seven per cent comes from the words actually spoken. Several experiments have been conducted where an audience is shown a TV segment – an interview or a debate – with the sound turned off. The viewers then make up their minds about the credibility of the interviewee or the winner of the debate. [One of the earliest and most famous examples of this phenomenon was the Nixon-Kennedy presidential debate in 1960. Those who watched it on TV thought Kennedy had won. Those who heard it on the radio gave it to Nixon. The radio listeners preferred Nixon's deep, confident voice over Kennedy's nasal Boston drawl. They couldn't see Nixon's sweaty face and five o'clock shadow being shown up by Kennedy's cool handsomeness.] And it's very close to what they conclude when the sound is on.

I can imagine a time when we communicate without words. We already do.

Allan had the whole package. The telegenic looks. Good skin, good hair. The continuous ruddy complexion that signalled outdoorsman, not decadent lounging rock star. Blue eyes like a 1950s Hollywood leading man. The suits that were well cut but still manly and North American. Allan had all this, and the brains to underwrite it all. But Allan was so good at what he did that you actually paid attention to the words. And clearly, although I had never told Eli and never would tell him, as long as I lived, Allan had the best word man in his camp. But still, it was a visual medium, and the visual medium communicated clearly. Before Allan said a word, I knew he'd already won. I could see it in his eyes. He was about to change the game. And there was no losing in it for him.

He was relaxed. His eyes were clear. (I've always thought that Visine was one of God's greatest gifts to politicians.) He was wearing a light blue shirt, open at the neck, no tie. He looked like your very nice, very smart, very successful, but very down-to-earth neighbour in the kind of neighbourhood you would want to live in, just a little smarter, a little wealthier, and a little better-looking than you. Just enough so that you respected him for it, not so much that you were jealous.

"Hello, Canada." The right tone of cheery. "Thanks for giving up your time today. I have something important I want to talk to you about. We have a wonderful country, as you know. It's something I've always believed. Times are challenging right now, but we have a lot going for us. But that's not what I want to speak with you about today. I need to apologize for something I said, something I said in private.

"Now, before I go on to tell you what I said, I want to tell you that you are going to get a real apology from me. None of those usual political or corporate apologies that have been so tortured by lawyers or spin doctors that their mothers wouldn't recognize them. I'm not going to shift the blame to you with 'I'm sorry if I offended you with my remarks.' I'm not going to do a poll to tell me if I should apologize. I'm not going to scan the editorials in *The Mail and Post* for tips. I'm not going to ask my people to visit the chat rooms of the nation to see if the story has legs. I'm not going to be grudging or defensive. I'm not going to blame an aide for doing or not doing what they were supposed to. I'm not going to try to give you additional context or explain that what I really meant was X, not Y.

"I'm not going to tell you the media are out to get me. I'm not going to tell you I overdosed on my cold medication. And I'm not going to pinch myself out of sight of the camera and cry. I'm not going to tell you the Opposition reaction is insincere. I'm not going to tell you that the stress of the campaign got to me, or that I'm concerned that the Opposition's attacks are getting to our supporters.

"The fact of the matter is that I screwed up, plain and simple. Earlier this morning, I had a call from a reporter. I won't say who it was. It doesn't matter. It was early, and he wanted a comment. I told him I didn't have one at the moment, but agreed we might talk later in the day. I hung up my phone." Dramatic pause. "Or at least I thought I did. But I left my BlackBerry on. And then I spoke to the person I was meeting with. And I said some things about all of us as Canadians, and how we are not always grateful for everything we have here in Canada. That despite the current economic crisis, which I know is causing pain and worry, we still have it better than most and that everyone has to adapt to new economic realities and that we should stop our whining." He looked pained as he said that last word.

"And now I'm not going to tell you how my family has served Canada for generations, or how my mother grew up hungry in a flat with no heat, or how my grandfather was a union leader who worked hard every day to help make Canada a better place. I'm not going to tell you how I feel about Canada and Canadians, how this country holds a special place in my heart. As you all know, people say the strangest things about their wives, their husbands, their children, their parents. But that's no excuse. I take the blame for what I said. I am truly sorry.

"I've always believed that politics is an honourable calling, and that there are many easier and many harder ways to make a living. I've always understood that politicians, especially in this day and age of the 24-hour news cycle, are held to a higher standard than almost anyone, except for maybe hockey players and priests," – he permitted himself the faintest of smiles – "and I've always believed that a man without integrity is not worthy and does not deserve to serve. In less than seventy-two hours, this country will be making a choice about the future. I understand that our government's fate is in your hands."

Less than ninety minutes later my Google Alerts picked up "Mog's Blog." Written by Susan Mogley, it was the most widely read political blog in Canada. With every sentence I became more nervous and wanted to stop reading, but of course I couldn't help myself:

> Every so often one of those moments happens that makes everything around us a little clearer. All of us in Canada experienced one of those moments today when we were reminded that we have the best political leaders in the world.
>
> Earlier today our PM admitted that he said some things about working Canadians, things frankly that all of us have thought at one time or another but have been afraid to say. Well, our PM said those things. That he happened to say them to a journalist when he thought he'd disconnected his BlackBerry doesn't change a thing. (The BlackBerry actually wasn't his, but more on that later.)

The initial response from my fellow brothers and sisters-in-arms in the news media was predictable. How dare he say such things? How hypocritical! How insincere! How can the man who pretends to speak so highly of Canadians harbour such narrow-minded (one scribe actually used the word "bigoted") sentiments? "The PM bared his secret soul, and it is dark," blared the purple prose on one radio station. In fact, the only ones who are hypocritical here are those of us who build up and then knock people off their pedestals for sport.

We often joke that we get the politicians we deserve. And it's true. We also get the journalism we deserve because in the end, people have to buy what we write or put on the air. And we're a funny lot, us journalists. We uphold the highest standards of truth and justice on behalf of our readers and viewers. Nothing gets our juices flowing more than to expose lies and untruths. We naturally assume that for certain professions the truth is a more elastic concept than it is for the rest of us.

All of us, of course, expect those who seek and hold political office in this great country of ours to tell the truth. But the real truth is that the only thing our society enjoys more than eviscerating those who lie to us is the very special punishment we reserve for those who tell the truth. Especially unpleasant truths.

We are all the descendants of the grand inquisitors who would put women on trial in the Middle Ages, maybe because they enjoyed the company of black cats, or were lesbians, or talked back to their husbands. The judicial process was, "We'll tie you and your kittens to a fifty-pound weight and throw you in the river. If you float, you must be a witch, so we'll dry you off and burn you. If you sink, well, you're obviously not a witch so, by the time we retrieve your body, we'll send you off to the great second act in the sky with a proper Christian burial."

Does anyone remember Kim Campbell when she innocently – and correctly – commented that elections were no place to discuss serious issues? Does anyone remember the last politician who admitted that he – yes, politicians are still usually he's – just might actually have to think for one second about raising taxes to slay the deficit? We are the ones who are the hypocrites.

Before we vote later this week in an important election – important by virtue of so many issues, that some nevertheless would have us believe is about what one man said when he was in the privacy of his own office – think about this: how many of us would want our character judged on what we say in the close company of our spouse, lover, friend, or colleague?

We might think what someone says in his private life should be no different from what he says in his professional life. I say fiddlesticks, we are human. And journalists are not superior in this respect. You'd be surprised if I told you that some of my most-loved, celebrated, and sensitive colleagues made the darndest sexist remarks in the company of those they trusted just hours before going on to write award-winning stories about gender equality in the workplace.

You'd be shocked to know that some of my colleagues routinely tell the most macabre, offensive, and, yes, funny jokes about the latest casualty in Afghanistan – I won't divulge the most recent example other than to say it involved IEDs, the Taliban, and a new twist on why the chicken crossed the road – just hours before filing heartbreaking, superbly written stories articulating the grief felt by a mother and father when their only son goes off to war and returns just days before his tour of duty ends, his body in pieces.

We all like to think we are above the fray, that we are more sophisticated and enlightened than the good burghers in Salem or the party bosses in Soviet Russia, or the thought police in Orwell's *1984*. But which one of us would knowingly enter a profession that has more stress and pays a lot less than so many others when every thought, every private conversation – and every expression of humanity, of personality, of humour, of individuality – was fair game? Only saints or those extremely twisted would apply.

There's one other point here that deserves mention, and that's the quality of the PM's apology. There's nothing I find sexier and more appealing in a successful male politician than a good strong, masculine apology. No tears, no excuses, no fuss, just the facts. As the overused expression goes, but one that is entirely appropriate in this case, he took it like a man.

And, to complete the picture, he scored even more points in my books. You see, I have it on good authority that the mistake with his BlackBerry wasn't his. It was his deputy director of communications who neglected to end the call. And the deputy director was with the PM, because the PM had told, practically ordered, Eli Tredman, his director of communications, to take a day off in the campaign – which is simply unheard of; this is a time of war for these guys – to visit with his dying father. When was the last time a great man took the deep, long, dangerous fall for his aide? It's usually the other way around.

Do any of us really believe there is someone in Canada who understands ordinary Canadians – and I use that slightly pejorative term reluctantly for want of a better one – more than our PM? The PM made the kind of statement a man might make about his wife if he truly loves her but is exasperated by her working late yet again. We reserve those moments of unguarded honesty not for those for whom we secretly harbour contempt, but for those we love the most.

As someone who once had the privilege of running for office (I lost by a whopping 4,900 votes, and I think only my mother and my then-boyfriend voted for me) I can tell you that the job of a reporter – afflicting the comfortable and comforting the afflicted and standing as the last soldier on guard for democracy against the barbarians – is a tough, glorious, unglamorous, important job, and one that doesn't pay nearly enough. But I can also tell you, as a linguistic Tithonus who has been on both sides of the microphone, it is easier to be asking the questions than answering them.

As hard as writing is – Hemingway once described the process as sitting down every day in front of the typewriter and bleeding onto the empty page – it is more difficult, and riskier, to act than to write, to be up balancing on the tightrope than down in the audience trying to capture the experience in words for everyone who was at home watching TV or putting their children to bed.

And then the Prime Ministerial tweet appeared:

I made a mistake today, and I'm sorry. There's not much more I can say. To view my apology, please visit www.youtube.com/watch?v=55fQnXMe7.

ELI

The Leader of the Opposition was impeccably dressed, as always, in a tailored suit that was probably just a little too tailored. He got away with it because he was, as the well-worn expression goes, a real man's man. Maurice Jonquière had grown up in Anjou, the son of a grocery clerk, was drafted and played three years of professional hockey, then earned a scholarship to Harvard. He still played regularly on a recreational hockey team, bench-pressed three hundred pounds, and had the God-given grace of an athlete. You could often find him – and photograph him – playing touch football on Parliament Hill. To complete the perfect picture, he was happily and very publicly married to Marie Tremblay, a TV personality who was more popular in Quebec than the Virgin Mary and Céline Dion rolled into one. When I called him that morning, right after speaking with Susan Mogley, he was at first surprised to hear from me.

"Good afternoon," he said to begin his press conference. "Thank you for being here with us today. I am here to officially respond on the part of the Opposition to the Prime Minister's unprecedented apology. Today, our Prime Minister did not equivocate or pull any punches. He came completely clean with his unguarded comments about working Canadians who are currently struggling to make sense of the economic meltdown, of a financial system that failed us, and who are also struggling to make ends meet. With his comments, the PM opened a dark window into his soul. And I must admit, it was not the prettiest sight." Maurice paused here, with the professional politician's sense of timing, as equally beautiful to behold as a forward holding onto the puck for that fraction of a second longer than most of us would, waiting for that perfect opening to slip the puck between the goalie's pads.

"But with his apology, the Prime Minister took responsibility. Let me be clear: the Prime Minister and I have been opponents, politically speaking, for many years. We have disagreed on almost everything, as you well know. But we have also had one thing in common: both of us care deeply about the future of this great country of ours and about the well-being of all Canadians. Today, as I can well understand, there are many who expect me to go for the jugular, to oppose, to cry 'Shame,' to call for the Prime Minister's resignation." Pause. "But I am not going to do that today. Too often our politics in this beautiful country descend into manufactured outrage, petty squabbles, inconsequential debates about insignificant details. I am not going to do that today.

"The Prime Minister I know, despite being my opponent in the political arena, is a committed man, who has chosen public life to improve the condition of ordinary Canadians. I thought his apology today, not the quick, unthinking words uttered in the privacy of his office early this morning, showed his true character. None of us is perfect – it would be a dull world if we were. And because of that, I accept his apology."

As he finished his speech, I felt Maurice looking directly at me, through the camera, through the TV, into my eyes. And I knew that I made exactly the right decision years before, when one late night in Quebec City I saw him coming out of a hotel room like an innocent deer onto a highway.

MICHAEL

That afternoon, at our editorial board meeting, my paper decided to kill my story. Comments on our online edition were running four to one in favour of the PM. The story I was asked to write instead was how political opinion was shifting and how the PM's gaffe, already affectionately dubbed "BlackBerrygate," was going to bounce right off him and have zero bearing on the outcome of the election. My editor, whom I'd worked with for years and with whom I was friendly outside of work, was sympathetic to me. But our new editor-in-chief, who was five years younger than me and who fancied himself a burning apostle of the new media, stared at me the way you might look at a senile aunt in a nursing home: with a mixture of pity, disbelief, and horror. He couldn't forgive the fact I had played by the old rules. I gave Eli a good old-fucking-fashioned print publication deadline. And instead of working hard to meet it, Eli created his own story and made his own winning move.